MW01065078

# LOST VEGAS

# LOST VEGAS

## Ron Uselton

To order additional copies of this book, contact:
Xlibris Corporation
1-888-795-4274
www.Xlibris.com
Orders@Xlibris.com
29722

To Beth

# Chapter One

Mid-afternoon; Flamingo Road and Las Vegas Boulevard: the busiest intersection in the *civilized* world, unless, of course, one defines "civilized" as Oxford might. "Advanced stage of social development; polite and good-mannered; refined"—not Vegas; not ever.

On that peculiar afternoon, horns were blaring and bleating like an immense automotive orchestra tuning up for the evening's overture.

"A cacophony," Spike "the Word" Spivey said, searching out and nailing the word for the day. Spike gripped the wheel of his black P.T. Cruiser with one hand while holding onto the top of his skull with the other, the sounds a tangible force, trying to pry it off. Even in that position, and seat belted, Spike still emanated the illusion of constant motion, bubbling like carbonation. That's not to say he was "bubbly." Debbie Reynolds is bubbly. Spike bubbled more like the release of a noxious gas, or lava at a fissure of the earth.

"The very word I was thinking," Oxxie Bozone said with a smile. "*Car*cophony? Like . . . a car symphony." He was fanning out his most recent acquisitions like poker cards in his enormous hands: a pink, two yellow, and one red-white-and-blue magnetic "Support Our _____" ribbons from the trunks of tourists' cars. Bozone had no idea how many he'd collected, but he'd let the nail on his pinkie grow out so he could pop them off their resting places quickly and quietly.

They sat in front of a line of two mile gridlock, facing north on Las Vegas Boulevard, the watery wonders of the Bellagio spraying at their left and the moving sidewalks of Bally's soaring to the right. Moments earlier, a firetruck had snaked around the traffic on Flamingo to cross the intersection. Cars were lined back in each direction for miles, their front lines like armies, met at Armageddon. Traffic lights were red in all directions. And stayed red, and stayed red, and stayed.

"You know, it's your fault," Bozone said, watching the unchanging red light, and Spike did know. "You and that microwave thing."

Spike reached up on the dash and grabbed the microwave transmitter he'd bought on Ebay. It was the same system that emergency vehicles were equipped with, to change the traffic signals. There was nothing Spike hated worse than sitting at a traffic light. Waiting was not his forte. The device worked, but, apparently he had activated the thing while the firetruck was activating its own, and the traffic signal, suddenly bombarded by different commands, simply shut down completely. Horns howled, and Spike gripped the wheel tighter, the delay like fingers squeezing his heart, but refusing to move his precious cargo against the light; an the RV at his right, the driver in orthopedic wrap-around shades; Bozone was eyeing the star-spangled "Support Our Troops" magnet on the RV's side.

"Why don't you . . . ease on through?" Bozone suggested, nudging the air with the back of his hand.

"Don't want to draw attention," Spike said, staring forward, as an air horn blasted three cars back and Spike lost his sunglasses in a flurry as his fingers tried to grab them. Spike swirled around in his seat toward the endless line of cars behind him, glanced above to where the pedestrians were crossing on overhead walks, "Look," he said, "here's what we do," squirming, his features pinched even closer together, he turned back to face Bozone. "Get out, go over to that crosswalk, push that pedestrian button and the whole system will reset."

Bozone looked at Spike squarely in the face. That could only happen while they were seated. Spike was a condensed crook, his features as terse and vivid as his personality: black, beady eyes, a lipless mouth and the whole face hatcheting down to a knife-like nose. A nose, that, at the moment, had a bead of sweat about to drop from it. Bozone was a broad, clean plain.

"Go," said Spike with a flick of his tongue to his upper lip. Bozone knew what to do when Spike used his reptilian tone. Maybe bloodshed would follow, and, whether it turned out to be his or Spike's, for the sake of argument, he opened the door and unfolded himself to his seven foot height, clicking the magnetic ribbon off the RV as he stood.

Bozone hadn't grown an inch since middle school, where he'd towered over classmates and teachers alike, but he'd cultivated his girth since then. His chest was as wide as a pier, which caused him to have to stoop *and* turn sideways to maneuver most doors, and his shoulders looked like he was dragging an ox-yoke plow. Thus the name, Oxxie. His father, long since homeless and probably pigeon food by the time Oxxie finished high school, had told him in a boozy taunt, "you coulda been a pro forward!" But Oxxie hated the game, all games, preferring the self-sufficiency of his infinite collections and his time alone to the ruthless togetherness of team sports. As close as he came to truly capitalizing on his size was when he put on a homemade ape suit and ran through a forest clearing so two documentary film makers he'd met on a fishing trip could get famous with a 45 second shot of Big Foot. His shining moment came, halfway through the clearing, when he slowed and turned to look at the camera. He'd had to turn his whole body instead of just his head, so he could see through the eye holes in the hairy mask. It made a very realistic impression.

"Amazing," the film analysts hypothesized, "big bipeds like apes can't turn their heads like humans. They have to turn their torsos. These pictures of Big Foot must be real!"

He kept the costume, but never got to reprise his role.

Oxxie reached the curb in three lopes and pushed the walk button. Instantly, the traffic light turned green, all the traffic lights, in every direction, even the arrows for the turn lanes. Spike patched into the intersection without looking either way and without waiting for Oxxie to get back, and was hit in the right front panel by a monster Olds patching from the right and in the left rear panel by a jack-rabbiting gypsy cab, spinning him 180 and cracking the Cruiser like an egg shell.

What happened next is one of those stories that really needs to stay in Las Vegas.

When the Cruiser cracked, a black plume sprayed up, like bumblebees leaving their nest, and then lay down like a dark shadow over the concrete of the intersection, a huge black comma. The world sucked in two short breaths, two silent beats, eyes widened, and then complete pandemonium ensued. People were out of their cars from every direction and down on the 120 degree street, fighting in huge, fleshy, sweaty blobs for the hundreds, thousands, of black $100 chips spread over the ground. There were reports that one very large woman jumped from an over-head walkway to join the war, breaking a leg, and the arm of another pedestrian as she ripped the chips from his grip. Children were reported missing. Family pets disappeared without a trace. Sirens wailed. Cars were left abandoned, never to be reclaimed. Bare-breasted women were everywhere, their tops ripped off, some of whom had been in the fray. One elderly couple was found in a nearby casino, addled, confused, oil-stained, and trying to cash in a radiator cap. The woman was holding a yellow, magnetic ribbon.

When Spike first saw the plume of black chips splash into the street, he said, "uh oh," flicked his tongue to his upper lip, got out of the Cruiser, reached back in, took out the microwave transmitter, and walked off, up the Strip, with that strange jolty walk of his that looked like a race-horse twitching off flies. Oxxie fell in behind at a safe distance.

# Chapter Two

Audra Sue patted and poked the last piece of her worldly belongings into a twelve dollar suitcase she'd bought at the Marcusville, Oklahoma dollar store, complete with pop-up handle and plastic wheels, and then zipped up the sides. She hefted the wheelie off the bed, set it upright on the floor, then smoothed out the ripples on her knobby bedspread. Then she sat on the bed and cried again, hating herself for wasting time on the tears.

The tears weren't for him, or what he'd done to her. Those had been cried and dried. Audra Sue was scared. For the first time in her young life, Audra Sue was about to step off into space: to do something so outlandish, so out of character, that it terrified her. She was going to leave the little town, her old world, where she'd started grade school, where she'd received her high school diploma under the same roof; the town where she'd buried her mother. She was going to leave the friends she still had after she'd ignored their advice and married Bill, the few that had stayed after the post office closed and the downtown square stood vacant and grey with decay. She was about to set out: alone, unsupervised, untrained, and mostly unfinanced. The $2500 she had scratched together from cookie bowl savings, her last check from the insurance agency, and pawning her wedding rings seemed a huge lump at the bottom of her purse, but she knew it wouldn't last long.

Married *five years* to Bill. Audra Sue involuntarily shuddered every time she said it. But, it had all come unmercifully loose two evenings before. Audra Sue and Bill were spending a rare night out at a local fast food café, celebrating a successful poker night for Bill or somesuch, when a tall woman with big blond hair walked up to Bill. "Aren't you going to introduce me?" the blond said.

Bill swallowed his lump of hamburger meat, a face like he'd just swallowed a can of varnish. "Uh, Mazie . . ."

*Mazie!*

"Uh, this is my wife, Audra Sue."

They nodded toward one another. To an observer it might have looked like the nod before the referee started the fight. Audra Sue with a question on her face, Mazie with a smirk.

"Audra Sue!" Mazie said. "I've been wanting to meet you! Bill says your name a lot while we're having sex."

Blackness encircled her vision and closed in. She felt like she was looking out a drain pipe with black sludge pouring in. Then she was on the floor with a damp wash cloth on her forehead. As soon as she opened her eyes and figured out where she was and that the nightmare she'd just had was not a dream at all, she ripped the cloth from her head, rushed out the door in an embarassed crouch, and ran the two miles to the trailer.

That night she lay in her bed, eyes staring at the ceiling, silently gesturing to empasize her thoughts, and planning what to say, exactly what to say, when Bill got home. But he never did. The next day she quit her job, hocked her rings, packed her bag, and was about ready to step out into space. Scary.

Audra Sue twisted a tissue into her eyes and got up to look at herself in the mirror. Her face was a mess, but she could work on that. Her hair, soft, auburn and shoulder length, was tied back, accentuating her porcelain skin. "Maybe need a little sun," she whispered. She put her hands flat at her ribcage and slid them slowly down her sides and over her hips. "A little too thin," her mother would have said. Audra Sue had on a faded pair of jeans and a tucked in, western style snap button shirt. She pulled the shirt tails out of her jeans, unsnapped the bottom two buttons, and tied the tails in a knot at her waist, emphasizing her slender midriff and her moderate-to-generous breasts. Audra Sue cocked her head, took one more look before she turned to leave, and smiled. "Maybe I'll get a tattoo," she said.

# Chapter Three

"Scary," Alex Sharp said, swaying, not bending, his 507 pounds forward to peek over the edge. The sky was dark, but, 175 feet below, the street was lit with a zillion tubes of multi-colored neon, and, more directly below, a huge kidney-shaped pool glowed a startling shade of blue.

"All you gotta do," the kid name-tagged Jimmie, with a lop-sided smile and a smell of hashish, shouted over the wind, "is stick your toes over the edge, arms out in front, and then dive." He demonstrated. "Step out into space," he said.

Alex reminded himself of the sign before he had entered the rocket-shaped elevator: "One bungee jump is as dangerous as driving 100 miles in an automobile." Highway death statistics flashed through his head. Oriental women drivers. Elderly men wearing fedoras.

Somewhere below he heard a high-pitched squeal. He couldn't make out the words, but he knew they must be shouted encouragements from the woman who had dared him, nay, *bribed him* with sexual favors so rare and delicious, that he stood on a platform, bound around the waist and chest with thick rubber ropes, his champagne buzz quickly fading, replaced by a dull headache. "No 50 year old man should ever have to do this," he said.

"What?" Jimmie asked, cupping his ear to hear.

"Nevermind," shouting, "how close will I get to the ground?"

"Some dudes your size actually graze the pool water," Jimmie said, awed by the possibility. "Righteous event!" Jimmie bounced up and down on the balls of his feet in the cooling night air.

Alex didn't move a muscle.

But, then, a sound drifted up from the night: words so tempting and tantalizing that Alex's nerve, and the bulge in his pants, grew in tandem. A phrase that confirmed his belief in God and got him walking toward the edge all at once.

**"36 Triple D!"**

Jimmie was wrapped in a blanket near the bungee pay booth, trembling and sipping coffee, like *he* was the victim, instead of the recently deceased Alex Sharp. Harrison Finch pulled up a folding chair and sat next to him.

"Jimmie Taylor?" Finch asked.

"Right." A shudder, like being Jimmie Taylor at that moment was pretty damn frightening.

"I'm Detective Finch." A pretty frightening guy. A triangular body, upper torso bulging out of a thin, white dress shirt, no tie; so black his bald head shone like obsidian quartz. Harrison Finch had been with the Las Vegas force for ten years, and L.A. another 12 before that. He had to leave L.A. because he killed a kiddie-porn photographer, in broad daylight, on a Wednesday, in front of City Hall. That caused some folks to call Finch a hero; others called him just plain mean. Some called him opinionated, but all of them had to call him long-distance because the L.A. police already had enough police brutality lawsuits to wallpaper the court house. Vegas liked his style. The pornographer had a thing for children and their pets.

"What happened?" Finch asked.

Jimmy sniffled and started, shakily. "Through no fault of my own . . ."

"Whoa there," Finch raised a calloused palm. "Last time I heard anybody start like that, they were explaining why my cat lay dead in the driveway. Just tell me what happened."

Breath after every phrase. "Guy came up, big guy, I strapped him in, he dove off. Next thing, I hear a sound, first a whap, and then, like a hollow *thump*." Jimmie turned to his left and threw up, then turned back, with a weak smile. "I looked over the edge and just then the cables snapped back up and nearly clobbered me."

"Dangerous job," Finch said. "Anybody with him?"

"Huh?"

"A little unusual that someone would bungee jump alone. Isn't it?"

"Maybe. Usually two or three guys or a couple. A few go off alone. I'm not sure he was alone. Someone may have been at the bottom egging him on. That happens a lot."

"Did you see someone?" Finch asked.

The kid shrugged. "Didn't make much sense."

"What?"

"Never saw no one, but I heard something. Woman yelled 36 Triple D."

"Hmmm." Finch said. "We might have a partial description." He patted the kid on the knee as he stood up. "You take it easy. I'll probably need to talk to you again."

"So," Jimmy said, "you investigating the accident for the hotel? Because, I swear, I strapped him in real tight."

"I'm sure you did, Jimmy. I'm sure you did." Finch got up and started toward the pool, its blue waters stained a pale purple. "You hear or see or remember anything you call me, Jimmy," Finch spoke back over his shoulder. "I'm in the homicide division."

Jimmy turned to his left and threw up again.

The body lay on the side of the pool, covered by a wet sheet. A photographer and a tech stepped aside. Finch pulled back the bloody end and took a first long look at the late Alex Sharp. His head was so flat, eyes bulging, teeth flattened, he didn't look real.

"He looks like a comic strip villain," the photographer said, leaning over beside Finch and aiming his camera. "Or maybe that flat-headed Frankenstein monster."

Finch swivelled his neck around and glared at the photographer until he blinked and stepped aside. Finch had learned the art of the glare from his white, southern ancestors. He pulled the sheet further back, and estimated the vic's weight at 480-500, soaking wet, which he was, soaking wet. Finch noticed he was still wearing the harness, chest and waist, and made a mental note to tell Jimmy when he saw him. The contents of Sharp's pockets were in a plastic bag that Finch picked up and opened. Wallet with the usual I.D., 51 years old, Wisconsin resident, several hundred dollars in cash (not unusual for a Vegas visitor), several black casino chips, and a wet piece of paper that looked like Sharp had printed out an email.

Finch covered the body, and let his eyes run directly up the bungee tower. A rubber cord hung lifeless from the platform, so he located the rocket shaped elevator and rode to the top. Finch slowly hauled the cord in, using his hands instead of the electric pulley. It was a single, thick rubber cord, and, at the end, was what appeared to be a stretch break. The black rubber was stretched colorless, thinned slightly, and then there was a jagged tear.

"Rubber broke," Finch muttered to himself. "Those words don't mean nothin' but trouble."

# Chapter Four

We present, for your admiration and accolades, the ad-man extra-ordinaire. Equally at home in the board room or on the playing field, his forty/long physique would turn Adonis green. Columbia B.S.; Harvard M.B.A. Dressed in the latest fashions, a suit fit and cut in Paris and a tie hand woven by little fingers in Brazil, shoes aged and shaped by the artisans of Sweden, thick and elegantly greying hair coiffed by a carrot-top bisexual in New York, nails buffed by a velly polite oriental. A luxurious apartment in New York with a view of Manhattan and the park, and another in Vail, with a view of the slopes; a forty foot sailboat off the Vineyard, with a view of the water, but never enough time to use it. Debts like a corduroy turtle-neck around his throat. A nasty spot on his liver and an appointment to get a mole on his back biopsied. Never any better than his last idea.

J. C. Martin stepped away from the hotel mirror. The spin cycle in his stomach told him he was about to get his final shot; one last try. His last, rather, his *next* idea. Sweat speckled his upper lip. He had two strikes. This could *not* be his third.

That half-time fiasco was not his fault, it wasn't even his area of expertise, but it was laid like a dead rat at his doorstep. How do you control a couple of screeching, humping rock stars who know they're being watched by the whole world? He was sticking with the original explanation: "wardrobe malfunction."

Then there was the presidential candidate, again, not his specialty. All he did was tell the guy to get more "verbal" at his rallies, "one" with the crowd. How was J. C. to know that the guy was going to let out a blood-curdling "Yeeeeeehawwwwww" on a directional network mic that would forever resound in the annals of campaign politics?

Two strikes. On his way up the ladder he'd often marveled at his runaway success, thinking but not putting into words the thought that perhaps any skill he possessed was far outweighed by his extraordinary luck. Skill was cheap, Ivy Leaguers were a dime a dozen; he'd take luck anyday, and he'd had his share. Lately, however, the cards simply would not fall, and the golden boy at the Wall Street firm of Klinger, Steinmetz, and Rubicoff had to make a comeback. Or else.

Two months ago, Saul Rubicoff had summoned J. C. to his austere little office somewhere in the middle earth of the firm, the office where Rubicoff had started as a junior associate and had insisted on keeping.

"J. C.," Saul said, his bushy black beard streaked with a bit more grey since J. C. had last seen him, "I got a call from John North."

John North. J. C.'s father-in-law. Loving father to his wife of five years. The John North who just happened to be CEO of North Star Motors, an up and coming rival to the world's worst made and most driven automobile.

"He called me about the account," Saul said.

"Hrrmt." J. C. tried to process the information. The North Star account. "The" account. It was not "the" account, it was *J. C.'s* account. Always had been. He had earned that account, paid for it with five years of marriage to a constantly bickering botox grinch whose divine destiny was buying everything, at least once.

"Now, don't get me wrong, J. C., he wasn't complaining," Saul said, in a tone much too sonorous to sound sincere. "He was concerned. They have a new product about to debut, it's . . . uh . . ."

"One of their Japanese rat car creations," J. C. finished Rubicoff's thought.

"Yes, well, and they need an ad campaign to launch it." Saul extended his arms like he was bestowing a blessing, "And I told them that Klinger, Steinmetz and Rubicoff has total confidence in your ability to handle it. And we do, J. C., we do."

"Thank you, Saul."

Saul Rubicoff leaned across his stark, metal desk, so close that J. C. could see a sprinkling of lunch in his beard. "And if you screw this up, J. C., I'll have you dropped from a very high place."

The new addition to the automotive market was a small, two-seater, convertible pick-up truck—very small. To J. C., it looked like a golf cart with an attached flat-bed, like one of those little electric jobs used for nursery deliveries, but, it was a hybrid, a gasoline and electric powered vehicle that could go 1000 miles on a 15 gallon fill-up. Hybrid, to appeal to the yuppies. Pick-up, to appeal to the rednecks. Perfect blend, unless it appealed to *neither*, and that became J. C.'s objective, to establish an image that would call out to both types. Easy.

The debut was to take place at a gala ceremony at the Four Winds Hotel and Casino on the beautiful Las Vegas Strip, and J. C. started his campaign with a search for the perfect name for the car. That was not an easy task. He needed a name that would crystallize the cross-over, an environmentally friendly pick up truck for rednecks deeply concerned about the greenhouse effect. Hmmm. After weeks of wadded attempts, he employed a focus group.

Cletus Skinner was in the first focus group. A six foot something Texan from Amarillo, Skinner showed up in starched and razor pleated jeans, a snap button shirt with roses on the shoulders, and a black Stetson, which he refused to remove even when he sat in the little convertible. Getting into the car required Hindu joints and a non-sectarian lubricant, and, when finally encased, Skinner's knees were an inch from his cheeks. With his hands on the wheel, his arms were bent like crab legs, elbows jutting out at ridiculous angles, and his hat sat up above the tiny windshield. That was J. C.'s first mistake. Not the focus group, and not having big Clet participate, but, there was a security breach. Someone had a camera phone, and, the very next week, on the inside front cover of one of the nation's yellowest rags, the Rag, was a sneak peak of the new North Star offering, with Cletus Skinner inside, looking like a tarantula on a tick. "North Star Breaking Back to Market Midget."

But before that picture was even published, a second mistake was made; a mistake that would change the course of history. J. C. watched Cletus exit the car, amazed that he was able to stand, and noticed a round bulge in his back pocket. One of those funny little light bulbs with a pull cord appeared above J. C.'s head. From that serendipitous moment, the campaign had a direction, a course, a foundation upon which to build. "Luck," J. C. thought, "I'm back." From that instant, ad copy could flow, docu-dramas could be produced, artists could wet their brushes.

Several hectic days later, John North phoned. "I saw the picture in the Rag, J. C." That was all he said. J. C. knew North was alive because he could hear raspy breathing through clenched teeth.

"I've got things in hand, John. We'll be ready for Vegas."

"We're a laughing stock, son. 60 Minutes called; said they were doing an interview with the American Back Institute—offered equal time."

J. C. started to say that he didn't design the car; he started to say that it was a ridiculous engineering concept that no ad agency could salvage; he started to say that North had relied on him before and he hadn't failed him yet; he started to say something very personal about North's daughter, but, he had a quick flash of Rubicoff, looking a lot like a black-bearded Zeus, throwing him off the building, and he said, "Don't worry . . . Dad. Wait until Vegas."

"Wait? You tell me what you're working on *now*, J. C.!"

J. C. scrunched up both pair of cheeks and hesitated. It was like asking an artist to show his unfinished painting. "Well, I will tell you this much," he said, "what's the one thing a cowpoke's gonna have with him where ever he goes? It may be small, but it packs a punch? It's a necessity."

North was silent. "I don't know. His horse?"

"No no. Look at his back pocket. His dip, John. His tobacco. His snuff."

"Whatdaya mean?"

"His Copenhagen, his Skoal, his Kodiak, okay?"

"Okay."

"Wait until Vegas, John. I'm going to knock your socks off."

"Okay."

J. C. had a name for the little vehicle, and a name was where it all could build. A name that might remind a redneck of his dip, or a drinker of a German toast, and adding a little German to an automobile was never a bad idea.

J. C. left his room, took the elevator eight floors down, and slipped into the rear of the conference room on the second floor of the Four Winds. The room was arranged in huge concentric semi-circles. At the outer edge, long tables covered with white linen were stressing under elaborate ice statues and heated trays of exotic and semi-exotic food. Guests with nametags and some without were scooping lumps of Swedish meatballs and glistening crabmeat onto hotel plates. Next, there was a standing area, swooping between the tables and a central stage. Guests milled, shook hands, nodded, moved their mouths like they were conversing, and most were dressed in semi-formal evening attire, which seemed out of place on a hot Vegas afternoon. As he scanned the crowd, he saw John North, pumping hands and draining his scotch glass, and several other familiar faces from North Star and the press. J. C. spotted Judy North-Martin, his wife, the heiress, fawning over a tall trust fund baby with golden hair that cascaded over his never employed shoulders. Bart Conner was present, a reporter for Car & Driver, leaning real close to talk to a young red head, showing off a superb midriff in her jeans and knotted western shirt, probably a crasher, there for the buffet. Some big guy with a plastic sign in one hand nudged by them to take an eggroll from a heated tray. J. C. estimated maybe 300 to 350 present. Not bad. The core of the group were hand-picked journalists from some of the most influential automotive publications in the world. His stomach gurgled.

The lighting was on the dark side of low. Covering the stage was a semi-circular curtain covered with shiny sequins, and the stage lighting on the scaffolds that surrounded the stage were reflecting off the curtains to throw an eerie meteoric sparkle across the crowd and over the walls. It reminded J. C. of the lighting created by the mirror ball in a darkened skating rink.

The music started. Brass, mostly brass, announcing what sounded like either a bull fight or a space mission, and J. C. surreptitiously checked his zipper and headed for the stage. A microphone descended from the heavens to meet him there, which he took in one hand and began. A spotlight hit him.

"Ladies and gentlemen, on behalf of Mr. John North and North Star Motors, we welcome you here to the beautiful Four Winds Hotel and Casino on the spectacular Las Vegas Strip." The music changed to a happy, tinkling tune. "We're here today, as you know, to bear witness to an automotive marvel." J. C. tasted his breakfast at the top of his throat. "We're here today to be the first, the *first*, to witness a step forward in engineering, a step forward in urban design, a step forward in environmental concern." He had the crowd. "Are you a little bit country?" he asked. At that point, the first layer of curtain parted and a live country band complete with screeching fiddle and hollering steel guitar cut loose with a familiar hard-times tune about a failed crop or something as Billy Bob Benton, cowboy songster, began to sing. The crowd went wild. "Or a little bit urbanized?" said J. C., shouting over the song. Billy Bob stepped aside as a long, lanky black woman walked up, took a sensuous, gin inspired bow as the 350 present screamed like 2000, and did a half minute of her signature piece, a bluesy, jazzy, sleepy rendition of "Baby's Melancholic."

"Purina!" J. C. announced, pointing, as if everyone didn't already know.

The song trailed off and J. C. took a deep breath. So far, so good. Back on the mic.

"Whatever you drive, whoever you may be, we have the automobile for you. North Star Motors introduces the new, the dramatic," the inner curtain was rising and the crowd was hushed, except for Purina, who was loudly asking her bass player for something, J. C. pointed toward the little car, reflecting a thousand beams of light into the wide-eyed crowd, *we give you, the* "NORTH STAR . . . SCOLIO!"

A spattering of applause, then silence. Silence. A buzz around the hall: "Scolio?" Eyebrows raised toward one another. A titter of laughter in the back; a giggle or two on the side; and J. C.'s face turned to crimson as the whole room broke out into a drink spitting and tear drawing laugh. Big HA HA's. Huge rounded belly laughs. High pitched squeals. Even some knee slapping applause. J. C. stood in utter silence, an artery pumping at his throat.

Some said it was all intentional, aimed at making a laughing stock of John North and his rodent line of automobiles. J. C. would later blame it on a conspiracy by the art department, in league with a rival firm.

Ten feet away, on the spectator floor, also in silence but trembling, stood John North, eyes wide in pasty white circles like a racoon, mouth drawn into a tiny thin line, nostrils flared, hands balled into fists. He took three knee-locked steps to reach J. C. and voiced, almost reverently, certainly breathlessly, the question that was on everyone's lips that day and for many alcohol tainted hours to come. "**What were you thinking, son?**" were the last words J. C. would ever hear from his soon to be ex-father-in-law.

Somewhere in the back, Oxxie shook his head and said, "Scolio. The very word I was thinking."

The next day, the Rag reran the picture of Cletus Skinner under a front page headline: "CURVATURE CONFIRMED AT CASINO CONCLAVE." Underneath the picture of Clet, squeezed into the little car: "Look at my new Scolio, Sis!"

The Scolio, renamed "Southern Cross," never reached the dealerships. J. C. Martin, file-stamped "failure," barely reached the bar.

# Chapter Five

Mid-morning; Pennsylvania Avenue and E Street, J. Edgar Hoover Building, Headquarters of the Federal Bureau of Investigation, a month before "Scolio" became a late-night punchline.

Milton McMix tapped the glass of his wrist watch with his index finger and then checked the clock on his desk. He buzzed his secretary, "What time do you have?" She told him and he nodded. McMix seemed a small man, with a coal black wisp of thinning hair and Richard Nixon jowls. When he wasn't checking the time, he was grabbing his elbows to cross his arms against his chest as if it were freezing inside. It made him look like a corpse.

"Agent Riley," he said, to the young man he had summoned. "As Assistant Executive Under Secretary of Personnel," Phillip Riley wondered whether McMix maybe started every sentence with that phrase, maybe every thought, maybe every sexual act, but Phillip decided not to go there and sat down, giving McMix his best "I'm Not For Sale" look that the Bureau had taught him. "I have asked you here to discuss your new assignment," McMix said.

"First."

"What?" McMix looked genuinely confused, like he didn't recognize the word or who had said it.

"My first assignment," Phillip said.

"Uh, yes, your *first* assignment." McMix glanced at his watch. Phillip wondered how long it would take government work to make a McMix out of him. Milton McMix had a sterling record with the Bureau, but had advanced as far in his profession as even government service would abide. Perhaps a little too gung ho for even law enforcement, his career started to slip right after he sent a memo to the Director suggesting a secret handshake between the agents. "As Assistant Executive Under Secretary of Personnel, Agent Riley, it is my duty to tell you," Phillip had graduated near the top of his class, but figured from McMix's tone he was about to be assigned to the Antarctic, or Africa, or maybe Miami, and he braced himself, "we need you in Las Vegas."

Phillip dropped his chin, raised his brows, and stared. "Las Vegas? *The* Las Vegas?"

"The one in Nevada," McMix nodded.

"That's . . . a good thing," Phillip said.

"I'm quite sure it's not as bad as it sounds. It's just that . . . Mr. Riley, I'm sure you'll find me a bit prosaic when I say this, but Lost, rather, Las Vegas is a place of, shall we say, few rules, where it becomes quite difficult at times to separate right from wrong, good from bad," he shook his Richard Nixon jowls when he said those words. "Gooood from Baaaad."

Phillip suppressed a grin. He saw little Milty McMix, sitting in front of a twelve inch black and white T.V. in eastern Ohio, worshiping the heros in the white hats and popping his cap gun at the guys in black. "That's pretty much true all over, Mr. McMix."

McMix stood and walked across the room to stop and then restart the pendulum on the wall clock. He turned around and looked at Phillip Riley.

"Agent Riley," he said, folding his arms tightly across his chest, "I envy your youth." He crossed back to the desk and sat behind it, unfolding his arms and opening a small manila folder. "You have been assigned to an undercover task force combining our agents with Secret Service and local authorities. There's an ongoing investigation concerning counterfeiting and money laundering and what you're going to be doing for the next six to eight months is, well, gambling."

"Gambling?"

"In a casino. Gambling. Playing cards. On the government's tab."

"I can do that," Phillip said, nodding. "Can I win?"

McMix's jowls jostled in what could have been a smile. "You can take that up with the Four Winds Casino, I guess."

Phillip shook his head. "So my job is to sit in a four star casino, spending the government's money, gambling, ordering drinks? Is this some sort of an ethics test? A final exam? If I say I'll do it, do I lose my badge or something?" Phillip gave him his best "I'm Not For Sale" look in case he'd missed the first one.

"Ordering drinks?" McMix said, "no drinks," and shook his face. He tapped his wrist watch and looked through his window to see the digital time sign on the bank. "Good luck, Agent Riley."

"With the crooks or the cards, sir?"

# Chapter Six

Detective Harrison Finch sat in an elaborately embroidered chair in Victor Marcuso's elegantly furnished but modestly sized office at the Four Winds. The walls were covered in a light walnut paneling and lit at the top molding, throwing a cool glow across the deeply carpeted floors. Finch sat in front of Marcuso's century old desk, pocked and moddled by the apparent knife marks and gunfire of its previous owners, which sat before a tinted window that yielded a view of the courtyard pool, drained, scrubbed, refilled and shining like the bungee incident the night before had never happened.

"I hope you're not here to arrest any of our guests for indecent exposure," Marcuso said, filling two glasses with soft drinks at a bar surrounded by framed covers of the magazines he had published before he decided to build one of the world's largest casinos. Now he could be found on the cover of many of those magazines. A small, thin man, with grey combed back hair and a thin goatee with sharp dark edges, he was coatless and his white cotton sleeves were rolled up.

"Busted," Finch said. His eyes had been drawn to the assortment of thonged beauties on the courtyard since he'd sat down. "Maybe I'll just interrogate a few."

Marcuso brought a glass to Finch wrapped in the Four Winds logo. "I talked to Jimmy this morning and he's still a mess. He said the cord broke."

"That's the way it appears, Mr. Marcuso."

"Call me Vic. That cord," Marcuso said, walking back to his desk chair, "as far as we can tell we bought it from a local supplier and its test rating is over 1500 pounds."

"Is that enough for a 500 pound jumper, bouncing around?"

"I'd have to defer that question to our technical people. I'm thinking we should have posted weight restrictions, but Jimmy said the guy never bounced. Sounds like the thing just popped when he hit its full length. If it hadn't happened, I'd say it was impossible."

"Do you have security cameras around the pool?"

"Nothing to record the actual jump. They can run a video at the admission booth if the customer pays for it."

"And the customer didn't?"

"No. We have a few cameras at pool level," Marcuso said.

"I'd like to see the tape. The jumper may have been with someone; odd they haven't come forward," Finch said.

"You can see the tapes, but you may not need them," Marcuso said, tepeeing his fingers on the desk and watching Finch over them.

"Why?" Finch asked.

"Ever hear of Fitzlow Everhard?"

"The attorney with the shark-shaped billboards out on 15?"

"Unfortunately," Marcuso said, with a scowl like he'd bitten into a lemon. "A real gamester. I had a message when I walked in. He wanted to meet this morning."

"About the accident?" Finch asked.

"He didn't call it that."

"And you're going to meet with him?" Finch asked.

"My legal department would throw a fit, but, sure, I'm going to meet him. I want to hear what he has to say."

"Mr. Marcuso, Vic, this is a continuing criminal investigation, and . . ."

"You don't think I should see him either?" Mancuso interrupted, a little incredulous that he might not be a match for Everhard.

"No, it's just that, I'd just like to be present," Finch said. "I've got some questions of my own."

Marcuso looked at Finch and then nodded slowly. "I have no problem with that. Everhard might, and if he does, I still want to talk to him."

"We'll ask him."

"I'll call Everhard. Why don't you go stick some quarters in a machine or something. I'll have security notify you when Everhard's here."

"Will they know where I am?" Finch asked.

Marcuso smiled and shook his head at the massive black man. "Detective Finch, we have devices that can track a moth through this building. We can find you."

Finch left Marcuso's office and wandered around the edges of the main casino; finally relented and approached a five dollar blackjack table and tossed twenty dollars on the felt. The dealer, a young corn-rowed black woman with a weary smile, took the twenty and returned four red chips.

Only one other player sat at the table, and Finch's attention was immediately drawn by his haggard and ragged condition. He seemed a young man, probably still under thirty, with curly black hair that stayed on his head like a square cap. His eyes were tiny black coals surrounded by a network of broken veins and sunken into a pasty, puffy face. The only contrast in his complexion were the dark bags that encircled his lower lids. His mouth was a lipless, invisible line. He slouched over the table, elbows propping him up, keeping his face from crashing into the felt. He wore a white cotton long sleeve shirt that was so wrinkled it looked like unwadded paper.

"How ya doin'?" Finch asked, as he sat down.

The young man managed to raise his brow slightly in reply and give an almost undetectable nod.

Finch glanced at the dealer, who learned toward him and whispered, in a voice the other gambler could have heard if he weren't a zombie, "He's been here since the shift change at four this morning."

"Is he a local?" Finch asked, considering giving him a ride home.

"I don't know," the dealer said. "I see him here a lot."

The dealer dealt a hand. A 10 and an 8 for Finch. A 10 and a 4 for the kid. A King up for herself.

Finch audibly winced when he noticed the young man's bet. Seven green chips. $175 on a hopeless hand. And, sure enough, it was hopeless for everyone but the dealer. She flipped up an Ace and scooped up the chips with no enthusiasm.

The kid raised his bet to $350.

"He always so lucky?" Finch asked the dealer.

She nodded, sadly. She had seen the mark of the beast many times before— Las Vegas' dirty little secret—the gnawing, hollowing affliction of compulsive gambling. The casinos weren't built by it, but they certainly benefitted from it, and despite their feeble efforts to pass out 800 numbers to whomever might request help, they did very little to deal with the problem. Dealers saw the symptoms almost daily, and it ate at them, but their hands were tied to really do anything. Sometimes a dealer would suggest that a player cash out and quit, and such communications were not forbidden by the casino, but the hopeless cases still sat and pushed their chips, bought with hocked watches and next week's paycheck, into the dealer's rack.

The dealer dealt another hand, grunting as she hit a 20 and beat both players. The young man raised his bet.

"How much has he lost?" Finch asked the dealer.

She glanced behind her to see if anyone from the pit was listening. "Too much," she said.

At that moment a tall black suit approached the table and tapped Finch on the shoulder. Finch left his remaining $10 for the dealer, got up, and stepped around to the other end of the table. He put his hand lightly on the young man's crumpled shoulder. "I've got a meeting," he said, "but can I take you to breakfast when I get back?"

The young man shrugged off the hand and somehow stood up, palming his remaining chips. He gave Finch that "I'm Not For Sale" look that he'd learned at Quantico, and ambled crookedly off toward another table.

# Chapter Seven

Finch entered the office before Marcuso and the attorney were even seated. Fitzlow Everhard was a flash of teeth and tan and a white haired comb-over that bordered on the bizarre. If he was trying to emulate a shark, Finch considered, it had to be a hammerhead.

"May I take your cape?" Marcuso asked the attorney.

*Cape?*

"Thank you, no, Victor," Everhard said, unfastening a long shimmery thing from around his neck, spreading it carefully over the back of one of the embroidered chairs, and turning to Detective Finch. "And you are?" he turned and said to Finch, with a carnivorous smile.

"Detective Harrison Finch, LVPD. Mr. Marcuso invited me to this meeting."

"With your consent, of course," Marcuso added.

Everhard's brow furrowed and he blinked twice, visibly processing the data, then shined his teeth again at Finch and said, "Of course. Detective, you are most welcome to join us. I have never had anything to hide from the city's finest." Everhard was dressed in a light blue searsucker suit, navy blue shirt with white collar, and light blue tie with a tie-pin shaped like a shark. His belt buckle was a dollar sign and his tan, pony skin boots would pay Finch's rent for a month. The hands that had mesmerized a thousand juries were sparkling with rings, with big stones. Everhard could be any age, from 95 to 100.

Marcuso sat behind his desk as Finch took the chair nearest Everhard. The air smelled like honeysuckle with a hint of liniment.

"I guess we shall begin," Everhard said. "I represent the family of Alex Sharp, the poor man who suffered a most painful demise on your bungee apparatus."

"The family," Marcuso said, "a spouse, children, who do you mean?"

"Mr. Sharp was never blessed with children. He had a spouse, a very recent spouse, but one who's terribly distraught by his passing. Not only did she lose her love, her companion, her sole source of support, she had to watch it all happen with her own poor eyes—emotional trauma," Everhard stuck a stern finger in the air, "past, present, and future."

"Recent, you say," Finch asked, "how long ago was she married to Sharp?"

"What time is it now?" Everhard asked, glancing at a diamond studded Rolex on his wrist. "About an hour before Mr. Sharp plunged to his death. But they had been seeing each other all afternoon."

"The wife's name?" Finch asked.

"Her name is Mrs. Sharp," Everhard said, without missing a beat. "I have been asked to keep my client's full name and identifying information confidential at this time. She is a shy person; doesn't want the publicity. Shall we just refer to her as . . . 'the bereaved?'"

"Your client is a material witness," Finch said.

"Surely you will give her a moment to mourn her husband, detective. She will come forward at the appropriate time and tell you everything she knows."

"Uh, how big are her," Finch cupped his hands and placed them in front of his chest as Everhard's eyes grew wider, "is she well endowed, Mr. Everhard?"

Fitzlow Everhard jerked his head back as if from a bad odor and made a disgusted face. "Mr. Finch!"

Marcuso covered a chortle with a cough.

"We have a partial description and I'm trying to verify it," Finch explained.

"I'm sure your prurient curiosity will be satisfied when I tell you she is quite generously endowed, for whatever difference it makes. Quite generously. Now, enough of that."

"Mr. Everhard," Marcuso said, "what can the Four Winds do for your client at her, uh, time of loss?"

"Ah, Victor," Everhard began, "you've always been a man of very practical views. Of course, she'd like for you to turn back the clock, bring back her sweet Alex, but that is impossible. In the alternative, you must realize that a grave injustice has occurred, and that some entity, not an evil entity but one who was simply negligent, in breach of a standard of care that this great society and system of justice imposes on all its citizenry, to watch after and protect their paying guests," Everhard's arm swept the room, as if a jury, surely nodding off by then, were hanging on every word, "the self-same guests who build these palaces, who furnish these halls, and now, the cost of that wrongful death must be borne, and the pain and suffering, past, present, and future," he cleared his throat for all to hear, "and, in short, we want fifty million dollars."

Marcuso's eyes got wider than his face.

"But we'll take thirty five," Everhard added quickly.

Marcuso leaned back in his chair. It creaked. "Fitzlow," he said, the sound a bad taste on his lips, "I invited you here against counsel's advice so we could talk. I'm not admitting any wrongdoing, Four Winds *denies* any wrongdoing, but if Alex Sharp had family or other special circumstances, we would want to do whatever we could to help. I thought we could discuss those things and I was wrong. Instead, you have lived up to your long-earned reputation of being nothing but a bottom feeder." As if to prove that, Everhard's mouth began to soundlessly open and close like a carp. "Wait," Marcuso held up an open palm, "let me finish. I am going to make you an offer today and you can take it or leave it. You have until noon to decide. I just want to tell you that I am embarrassed to be part of a system that would let this situation develop, because we both know, even though your fifty million or your thirty five or some similar ridiculous demand for your client is absurd, our system allows a lady with just a coffee burn to hit the verdict jackpot and retire on someone else's earnings. The system belongs to unscrupulous and unethical remoras like you, I have grown to accept that, but let's get real, Fitzlow. The ink on your client's marriage license is still wet, and I'd say you might have about an hour in this case, legal time. Without waiving any rights of any other *legitimate* heirs or family, I'll settle your client's claim for $25,000. Noon today, it's off the table."

Everhard slowly stood up, the same slow and elegant rise he'd used to impress so many juries, anticipating his next words. "So, I guess we're through here," he said.

Marcuso nodded.

"Except I want to talk to your client," Finch said, handing Everhard a card. "I'll come get her if she won't come to me."

Everhard took his cape from the chair and folded it over his arm, a pained expression on his face, like the American flag had just been trampled by invading hordes. A jury-box tear in his eye. "I am sorry, Mr. Marcuso, that you feel that way. Twelve of Mrs. Sharp's peers may feel differently. A wrong must be righted. An injustice requires action." Everhard turned and walked toward the door, opened it, and just before he shut it behind him, he turned and said, "Noon, huh? I'll let you know."

"Bullshit," Marcuso said, when the door shut.

"Past, present and future," Finch added.

# Chapter Eight

Mikey "Don't Call Me Cheeso" Mozzarelli owned a ranch style estate conveniently close to a notorious bordello. A long, gated driveway curved up from a private road to a cactus spotted courtyard that was continuously observed by concealed cameras affixed to the house's wide eaves. Spike Spivey's rental sat in the driveway. Spike and Oxxie sat on stools at a granite kitchen counter top. Mikey sat on the other side of the counter top, slurping corn flakes. Mikey wore speckled boxer shorts, a wife-beater tee, and a light robe. His hairless, bulldog head was bent into the bowl.

"So, ya go inta da fuckin' casino, fuckin' siddown," pushing a soggy spoonful into his mouth, "buy da fuckin' chips," spitting soggy flakes.

"Brrrrmmbbbrrrmmpt." Spike said, having trouble keeping his words slow enough to be understood. "That's right," having to stress every syllable. "We go to different tables, buy ten, twelve thousand in black chips at a whack."

"A fuckin' whack?" Mikey pointed the dripping spoon at Spivey. "Dat's da word, Word. I oughta fuckin' whack da both of youse fuckin' screwups."

"OK, Mikey, you're right. Bad choice of word."

Oxxie nodded. "Not the word I was thinking."

"I fuckin' tellya, I fuckin' sez, take yer," for emphasis Mikey put down the spoon and pulled the next word between his fingers like he was stretching a strand of spaghetti, "tiiiiiiiiime. I sez, don't attract no fuckin' attention. Go to da fuckin' casino two, three times a fuckin' week. Buy in and cash out. Buy and cash. We're laun'drin da fuckin' money. It ain't a fuckin' speed wash!"

"Spike has a real hard time waiting for his shirts," Oxxie said. Spike glared at him with eyes that could freeze beef.

"Howja carry all da fuckin' chips?" Mikey asked. "Hunderd eighty large in blacks ain't gonna fit inno fuckin' shirt pocket."

"Bags," Spike said, "from the gift shop."

Mikey said, "Fuck."

"After we get the chips, I start noticing the casino suits may be watching us," Spike said.

"No fuck," Mikey said, "fuckin' tourists from Iowa wuz prob'ly watchin' you, rakin' chips inta fuckin' shoppin' bags. Pet poodles wuz watchin' you."

"We were getting some looks, so I motion to Oxxie and we go meet in a bathroom stall."

"Whereas *dat* location shoulda waylaid fuckin' suspicion."

"No cameras there, Mikey. I checked that out."

"Ask someone?"

"Uh huh."

"Fuck."

"We, uh, amassed the chips while in the stall and then I carried them up to this cashier. Trouble. Snappy little gal with an attitude. I stack ten, twelve thousand chips on the counter and I say, just like you told me Mikey, that we want a casino check. No cash—a check."

Mikey nodded. "Fuckin' got somethin' right." Mikey made a little circle in the air with the spoon.

"Little Miss Snappy goes, 'I gotta see I.D.,' for the reason that any payout over $10,000 they have to report."

Mikey nodded again and reached for the cereal box, pouring a fresh mound onto the remaining milk and then covering that with an equally large heap of sugar. Mikey took his spoon and jabbed it into the cereal, like he was wielding a blade in a motel shower or maybe like a spade loosening the fresh soil for a new grave. Maybe he was only trying to stir the cereal into the milk. Spike bit his lip and watched the spoon. "So whatja fuckin' do?" Mikey asked, "you ain't sayin' we *stuck* wid all dem fuckin' chips?"

Oxxie said, "No to that last part."

"I stepped away from the window," Spike said, prying his eyes from the spoon, "and I thought about sending Oxxie up there to say he was from Outer Mongolia or something and they didn't use I.D.'s in his country, but the clerk must have pushed some button or something because some suits began to definitely pay us some serious mind, so we regrouped back in the bathroom."

"Uh hmmm," Mikey said, "lots of ways to ex-cape from a fuckin' casino batroom."

"So, yeah, so we came out of there and separated and then met at the parking garage and then played hide and seek in there for a while with these casino dicks. But we got away."

"Fuckin' long shot. I woulda bet on da fuckin' dicks."

"I'm not sure they wanted to get us that bad. Can't figure what we'd done wrong, and Oxxie is a scary looking guy."

To prove it, Oxxie gave Mikey a fierce squint.

"But that," Spike said, "was where the real trouble started. We pull out of the casino garage and out of nowhere this big black stretch limo cuts us off." Oxxie gave Spike a quizzical look. Spivey looked him back, stone faced. "Cuts us off. Big guy with one of those machine gun pistols hops out and points it into

the car. Tells us to give him all the chips and then, Oxxie hands them over."
Spike turned to Oxxie and flicked his tongue to his upper lip, daring Bozone to
speak. Oxxie shook his head and kept his mouth shut, but the tongue thing was
looking more and more like a Cher impression and less and less dangerous.

Mikey placed his spoon in the bowl, soundlessly. Suspecting all along but
finally realizing that his hundred and eighty large was gone, Mikey asked, very
slowly, "What did dis fuckin' guy look like? Da guy wit da piece."

"I dunno," Spike said. "It all happened real fast. Dark eyes, nice suit."

"A black limo? Hmmm. And just dis one guy—no sep'rut driver. Did he
have a fuckin' scar on his right fuckin' cheek?" Mikey asked.

"I think so, yeah, he did. Right up there on his right cheek. A scar."

"And anudder scar cross his chin?"

"Maybe, yeah, I think so. I'm pretty sure."

"And wuz he missin' part of his fuckin' ear?"

Oxxie spotted a folded copy of the morning paper on the counter. On the
front page above the fold was a picture of a P.T. Cruiser surrounded by a crawling
mass of sweaty tourists; a headline about black chips spilled at the intersection.
Oxxie slipped the hopefully unread newspaper off the counter, tucked it under
his arm, and headed for the bathroom just off the kitchen. "Gotta go," he said.

"His ear. Yeah. Definitely, part of his ear was probably missing."

"Which ear?" Mikey asked.

Spike was silent, his miserable life flashing through his brain at a sickening
speed. He batted his temple with the ball of his hand to stop the slide show, and
flipping an imaginary coin, it came up tails! "His left ear."

"His fuckin' left ear?" Mikey said, "I dunno . . ."

"That was his left while *facing* us, Mikey. It would have been his right if we
were facing him."

Mikey made a rubbery sound with his lips and then slammed his fist down
on the counter top, either quaking the granite or at least flipping the spoon,
because Spike and the counter top and the wife-beater tee were suddenly dripping
with thick, sugary milk and wet, scab-like cornflakes.

"My fuckin' brudder in law!"

"What?" Oxxie said, returning from the bathroom, wiping his hands on a
towel that he flipped to Spike.

"Ya jus' got heisted by my fuckin' brudder in law!"

"Is that, uh, plausible?" Spike asked, rubbing the cornflakes off his forehead.

"It's downright fuckin' unbe*liev*able!"

Spike started to equivocate on the description but then Mikey said, "I
knew he wuz up ta som'ting, dat fuckin' rat fuckin' bastard. He swore ta me on
his mudder in law's grave dat he'd never touch my biz'ness on the Strip—
swore he'd keep his fuckin' int'rests downtown without no fuckin' fingers in

each udders fuckin' pie. I'll kill dat son of a bitch stealin' bastard. Ain't nothin' fuckin' sacred?"

"All I know, Mikey, is we had no choice. Bastard had us drawn down."

Mikey got up and crossed the room to look out through the kitchen's french doors at the scraggly desert garden in the back yard. "Listen to dis," he said, in a low growl. "I wan you shud bring me his fuckin' arm, the same arm dat held da fuckin' piece."

"His arm," Spike said.

"We'd probably have to kill him to do that," Oxxie added.

Mikey turned to them, his outstretched hand balled into a fist. "And I hope his cold fuckin' fingers are still graspin' my fuckin' black chips."

Spike and Oxxie made as quiet and quick a departure as they could and neither said a word to one another until they got in the rental and Spike started screaming at Oxxie and Oxxie told Spike it was all Spike's fault and they scuffled for each others throat in the front seat until Spike hit his balls on the gearshift knob and had to suck in a sharp breath and stay very quiet.

Back inside, Mikey raised his foot from a half inch of water on the kitchen floor, and yelled up the stairs, "Call yer uncle da plumber, Darla, da fuckin' kitchen toilet's overflowin'! And where's my fuckin' newspaper?"

# Chapter Nine

Little Bobby Crest sat in a barber chair at the mall smiling like a baby timberwolf. He'd been shampooed and trimmed, razored and layered, plucked and tweezed. His unibrow had been waxed into one segment over each eye. His nose had been rotored by a disgusting little circular saw and the little bursts of swamp grass that grew out of his ears had been carefully mowed. He could see all this handiwork in the mirror gloss of his new shoes. Cool!

The day was a new day for Little Bobby. That's what Vegas was all about: new beginnings, Little Bobby told himself, *Jackpots!*, as he hailed a cab for his meeting with Victor Marcuso, CEO of the Four Winds Hotel and Casino. Big Bobby would be proud.

Big Bobby was a distributor, a middle-man, a warehouser of what a growing Vegas needed when the desert rose only began to blossom. He came there with Little Bobby's mother in 1955 and started a business, a dream, called CrestLine, selling everything from hotel towels to Canadian slot machines and French gaming tables to a new but never fledgling industry, the gambling industry. He put it all together from scratch, locating and shipping goods from all over the world, storing them, creating colorful catalogs for potential purchasers, and then selling those items at good but moderate profits. He became the principal supplier for Vegas for nearly fifty years, long enough to put three kids through college and change wives like he was changing boots. His whiskered, cowboy appearance made him a favorite in the casinos until he finally died in his sleep three years ago, leaving a legacy of straightforward business dealings, high living, and an uncanny ability at cards, especially poker. Ask any of the old time players and they all had a Big Bobby story, always one in which Big Bobby won the pot because "it was like he could see our cards."

Little Bobby was the first of four kids, the only child by Big's first wife, and the only child that didn't go to college. Little Bobby remembered his early days in the casino, when children weren't even supposed to be around, when his dad would let him tag along and casino executives and even nightclub acts would rub his black, curly hair and say things like "a chip off the old block." Little Bobby grew up with that belief, that he was a chip off the Big block, that, one day, he'd make a dream a reality just like his dad, so he hadn't let little annoyances like regular employment or higher education get in his way. He lived in his dad's old house and he owned a piece of the old CrestLine operation, which had become nothing more than records stored in the attic, but he was really in the business of dreams, and he was searching for the big one that he could market, and then stroll through the casinos with a Big Bobby stride and a glint in his eye. And this was the day it could happen.

Little Bobby had learned that the dreaming part was not hard; the hard part was turning that dream into a reality. Which meant, convincing the right people. Nothing could be done alone anymore. In Big's day you could just set up a business, he told himself, and it would flourish. The good ol' days. Oh, to have his dad's opportunities. Now, he needed help, support, sponsorship, and, more than anything else, influence. He needed someone like a Victor Marcuso who knew all the ropes, *hell*, who owned all the ropes, and that's why Little Bobby had sent his prospectus to him. Now, barely two weeks later, Marcuso had called, requesting a meeting. Thank you, Las Vegas, for letting the Little inherit the earth!

Little Bobby got out of the cab in front of the Four Winds and walked in nodding hello to everyone he saw. In ten minutes, he'd be sitting in Marcuso's office, basking in the warm glow of fame and fortune. He laughed aloud. Everything's funny when you've got money!

His idea had come to him in an actual dream, a Sunday afternoon nap, but the concept seemed so obvious that he was surprised that no one had beat him to it. A major league baseball franchise! Vegas could support it, certainly financially, and the fan base was there. Whatever the team might lack in local ticket sales would be made up by tourist sales, a large part of which might be oriental trade (big enthusiasts of the game), and nearby cities following their own teams to the greatest resort city on earth. Boxing certainly thrived in the city, as did intercollegiate basketball. It's time for the great American sport to come to the great American city! Little Bobby even came up with a name for the team—the Greensox, symbolizing the desert oasis that Vegas had become and, of course, the Dollar, the life-blood of a growing Vegas. Little Bobby would get a small piece of the franchise for his effort, and maybe a part of the concessions. More than money, Little Bobby would earn the respect that he was due. Didn't a President used to own a ball team?

Victor Marcuso's secretary let Little Bobby into the office and seated him in an upholstered chair in front of Marcuso's desk. Marcuso was on a phone call and signaled that he'd just be a minute. Little Bobby leaned back, gave Marcuso a knowing nod between business giants and watched the thongs out the window.

"Detective Finch . . . Yes, Everhard called right before lunch . . . No. He said no to our offer . . . He said, how did he say that? He said, 'she's heavy with child' . . . That's right. Now he's claiming his client is *pregnant* . . . I know. Ours wasn't the only rubber that broke . . . Twelve hours. Gives a whole new meaning to early pregnancy detection. Could she know so soon? . . . Just be sure the coroner keeps a large enough hunk of Alex Sharp for a DNA test . . . I'll keep you posted . . . You do the same." Marcuso placed the phone in its cradle and sat behind his desk with a tired sigh.

"Mr. Marcuso," Little Bobby began, "you're not going to regret having me here."

"I don't know," Marcuso said, "I'm beginning to regret that the sun came up this morning."

Little Bobby laughed, and it created a hollow echo. "Uhmm," Bobby's eyes darted around the room, "so you liked my prospectus?" Little Bobby looked at Marcuso but he did a thing with his eyes. He had trouble with eye contact during close conversations, so he'd partially shut his eyes. The slight movement through the slits made it look like he was in a trance or maybe slot tumblers were going around behind the lids.

"Your what?" Marcuso said.

"My prospectus. A major league franchise. You know," Bobby cupped his hands to his mouth, "Cold beer! Cold beer!"

Victor Marcuso looked at Little Bobby Crest like he'd just dropped from the sky. Shaking his head, he said, "Are you sure you're in the right office? Food and Drink is down the hall."

*Food and Drink is down the hall?* It was Little Bobby's turn to look confused. "Mr. Marcuso," he said, concern beginning to pinch up his features, "my name is Bobby Crest. Your secretary called me this morning and set up this appointment."

"Crest. Sure, sure. CrestLine. You're the guy from CrestLine."

"Yes, that was my dad, you may have known him. I'm the son of . . . him."

"Several years ago, the Four Winds bought a bungee cord from CrestLine. I asked you here to talk about that. We found the old invoice in our file but we need the full list of specs. I understand you were the middleman, but surely you have access to the factory sheets, any test runs. As you may know, last night one of our guests . . . Mr. Crest, are you alright?"

Little Bobby Crest was turning magenta. A storm line of perspiration began to break out at the edges of his new haircut and rain down his face. There was a certain shortness of breath.

"I just . . . I just thought we were talking about something else."

"Do you need a glass of water?"

Little Bobby shook his head, knowing he'd spill it. "Haven't you read my prospectus?"

"Your what? You've got a prospectus on the bungee cord?"

"No no, not a bungee cord. I don't know any damn bungee cord. Have you read my prospectus on a major league expansion team?" The young timberwolf was beginning to growl. He was looking at Marcuso, eyes partly closed, eyeballs fluttering behind; he gave the impression of a man about to spontaneously combust.

Marcuso assessed his options. He could call security. He could plod on. He slid open his side drawer where he kept a stun gun. "Mr. Crest, I really don't know what you're talking about. If you've got a prospectus, I'll read it. But we've both got liability issues here and we need to discuss them."

Bobby raised his hand, as if summoning the gods of reason. "Wait. Okay. You may need to start over. I just had a . . . umm . . . I just thought this was about . . . start over."

Marcuso spoke very slowly. "We found the invoice on the cord we bought but it doesn't have any of the specs. We need those, preferably from the manufacturer."

"Actually," Little Bobby said, wiping his forehead with a clammy palm, "CrestLine was my dad's company."

"And you have none of the old sales records, catalogs, that sort of thing?"

"Well, maybe. The old files are in the attic," he said, "along with the spiders." His eyeballs fluttered through his half closed lids.

Marcuso's lunch began to taste raw in his throat. "Well, it may be asking a lot but we need to see the bungee cord papers. It's for your benefit, too. We're about to have a lawsuit here and I have no doubt CrestLine will be a party."

Another kick in the gut. Little Bobby opened his eyes wide. "There's nothing to get from CrestLine."

"Your dad didn't leave anything in his estate?"

"Well, the house I live in. That's about all. You don't think they'd try to take that do you?" Somewhere in the last few minutes Little Bobby had gone from magenta to completely colorless. The sweat still poured.

"Mr. Crest, with all due respect sir, if your dad's company misled us on those specs, *we* may try to take that."

Little Bobby Crest swallowed hard. "So, you said you'll read my prospectus." It was the only thing he could think to say.

Marcuso shook his head and put on a tight smile, "Send it to me."

Little Bobby stood up and handed Marcuso a stack of stapled pages. "Take this one. I'll, uh, go right now and look for those specs." He turned and walked toward the door, a few inches shorter and a lot less sure of foot than when he walked in.

Marcuso watched him shut the door and tossed the prospectus in his waste basket. Little Bobby heard the *plunk* in the outer office.

# Chapter Ten

Detective Harrison Finch checked the Clark County Marriage Inquiry System online but the marriage license had not been filed, so he let his fingers do the walking through over sixty wedding chapels in the yellow pages. He got his first hit at Mon Ami's Garden of Love and Dollar Store right off Las Vegas Boulevard, and headed out through the afternoon traffic.

Mon Ami's Garden of Love was a storefront operation in a small strip mall with elaborate gardenia blossoms painted on the front window. Finch entered a tiny reception area surrounded by flimsy Chinese partitions. He saw no one, heard canned music, so he poked his big head around the partition.

The room would make a cockroach run. The floor was the same sick linoleum in the reception area, those yellowish but mostly colorless squares inlaid down every middle school hall in America, but up the center of the floor, bordered by a few snaggle tooth rows of folding chairs, was a red and orange strip of shag carpeting that belonged in a dethroned middle eastern shah's temple. The walls were painted red and then flocked with a fuzzy felt substance that looked like a spore mold. An elaborate bronze chandelier with little naked angel bulb holders hung from a ceiling painted light blue with huge puffs of cotton glued to it. The whole place smelled like wet hair.

A small riser sat at the front of the room, where two very elderly people, the woman holding a plastic yellow "Support Our Troops" ribbon like a wedding bouquet, stood facing one another. A wiry, smiling man dressed in green overalls and a UNLV cap, turned backward, conducted the ceremony. A round, smiling woman sat in the front row with a cassette player in her lap.

Finch stepped back around the partition and waited until he heard a wobbly version of the wedding march and the two, slow-moving lovers came past the partition and exited the door. They were arguing over which buffet to visit for dinner. It was already 3:30.

Finch wound around the partition and found the green overall man sitting next to the round woman, splitting a small stack of greasy black casino chips.

The overalls stood. "May we bless your union, sir?"

"You may give me some information," Finch said, flipping his badge. "What's your name?"

The woman hit the reverse button on the cassette player and stayed seated. The man said, "Simon Peter Herkowitz. You want I.D.?"

"No need. I called earlier and someone told me you performed a ceremony late yesterday for an Alex Sharp."

"Yes. I think Alice answered the phone." Alice was nodding. The cassette player snapped to a stop. "I sent the license over for filing this morning," Simon Peter said.

"What I need to know is the maiden name of the woman he was with and a home address for either one of them if you have it."

Simon Peter took off his ballcap and rubbed his hand across his balding head, either wiping sweat or smoothing down phantom hair. "I dunno. I can give you the name she gave us, but we don't keep address information. Hang on."

Simon Peter flopped his hat back on, frontwise, and walked over to a short wooden pew against the side wall. He lifted its hinged lid. "Here it is," he said, "right on top." He picked out a slip of paper with a gardenia logo. "A name and a social security number. That's all we have to have." He handed it to Finch.

Finch read aloud, "Berta Mae Pole. You remember them?" Finch asked.

"Oh yes," it was the woman, Alice, who spoke up, "big ol' boy. Grinning like he'd stuck his hand down in the candy jar and never wanted to get it out. She was big, too, in all the right places if you know what I mean. I told Simon she's been in here before but he told me not to meddle." Alice gave Simon Peter a sour look and Simon nodded his head in silent affirmation.

"Well it's my job to meddle," Finch said. "No address, no phone number, no driver's license number, nothing else?" Simon Peter and Alice shook their heads in unison. "Did you see what kind of car they were driving?"

"They were in a cab," the woman answered as the man shrugged.

Finch thanked the couple for more information than he'd come in with and returned to his car. He climbed inside, started it and turned on the air conditioner, then stepped back out to use his cell phone. He called 411. Sure enough, Berta Mae Pole was listed. Shrewd detective work, that 411 call. Then he called the station and gave them the number and they did a criss-cross reference. It came up to an address on Charleston. He drove there, narrowly escaping a fender denting by the elderly newlyweds who were still slowly angling out of the parking lot.

The address on Charleston was a walkup frame apartment over an antique shop. Finch climbed the stairs to face a glass outer door, the tint so dark that he could only make out a faint glow inside, a woman, bent over so close to a laptop computer screen that it lit her features like a weak makeup mirror.

He rapped once on the door sill and said, "Berta Mae Pole?"

The face disappeared from the computer glow.

"Ms. Pole, I'm Detective Finch with the LVPD. Would you come to the door?"

"I'm not Miss Pole," a voice said in the dark, "I'm Misses Sharp. And I want my attorney here before I do any talkin'."

"*Well*," Finch thought, "*at least I found her.*"

"Ms., uh, Sharp, no charges have been filed. You're not a suspect for anything. You are a material witness, and unless the Supreme Court rewrote the Constitution while I was shaving this morning, you're not entitled to an attorney."

Finch let those words sink in, then continued. "As a material witness, I can take you in if you fail to cooperate."

"So, I've done nothing wrong but you can arrest me if I don't cooperate?"

Finch shrugged. "Yeah."

"What kind of country is this that the rights of a private citizen ain't worth no more than that?"

"The kind of country that would allow you to sue the Four Winds for fifty million dollars."

Berta Mae walked to the glass door and pushed it open. "We can talk, but I ain't signin' nothing."

# Chapter Eleven

"Plunk!:" The sound of the prospectus hitting Victor Marcuso's engraved leather bound wastebasket. The sound kept repeating in Little Bobby's head, like it was bouncing around in there and couldn't get out, like a .22 slug, he thought, in there, burrowing tunnels in his brain, seeking out neuron central so it could smash the bulb, shut down the systems. He felt raw, stripped of a layer of skin, vulnerable yet oblivious to everything around him. Aside from the fact that he'd just kissed rock bottom, part of his emotions arose from the simple embarrassment of being made a fool; the sharp edge of feeling worthwhile and being proved worthless. To hell with the prospectus—that didn't matter anymore. To hell with the Greensox. That's not the point. Marcuso could buy it or leave it behind. What hurt was that he'd been fool enough to believe that someone like Marcuso would give him the time of day. Little Bobby mimicked an overhead hoop shot. "Plunk." The sound of Marcuso's severed head hitting the wastebasket.

"I need a drink," Little Bobby said, aloud, gazing across the festive, excited, happy crowd of the casino, in their bright floral shirts and loud colors. He spotted a little Tiki bar in a far corner and shuffled, trudged toward it, avoiding eye contact as he went. He finally pulled himself up onto a black vinyl stool, motioned to the bartender and said "bourbon," who poured him a full glass and carefully set it on a napkin. Little Bobby took a long pull before he reached in his pants pocket and produced four wadded dollar bills.

The bartender looked at the money and back at Little Bobby. "Got a suggestion, sir," the bartender said, "that's a video poker screen on the bar in front of you. Stick a quarter in there every once in a while, and the drinks are complimentary." The bartender picked up one of the dollars and returned with four quarters. "That guy over there," the bartender said, indicating a man at the other end of the bar, "he's been drinking all day on a seventy five cent bet."

Little Bobby nodded and stuck one of the quarters into the machine, shoving his bankroll back in his pocket.

"Besides," a perky female said from behind him, "you might win a big jackpot and change your life." Little Bobby turned on the barstool to see a young auburn haired woman with china-doll skin in a very skimpy cocktail costume. She used both hands to grab her shorts where they met her mesh hose and jerk down.

"You can tell that Audra Sue is new around here," the bartender said.

Audra Sue said, "My daddy always told me to never trust a bartender with a red nose."

"My daddy *was* a bartender with a red nose," the bartender said, as Audra Sue then pulled up with both hands on her sequined, strapless bodice. "Girl, you're gonna pull that outfit apart!"

"I'm dressed like a meth whore," Audra Sue said, picking the shorts from between her buttocks.

"Designed to convince our guests they're not in Kansas anymore," the bartender said.

Audra Sue leaned across the bar, brushing Little Bobby's shoulder with the left side of her breast. "That guy's still here," she whispered to the bartender, cutting her big eyes toward the patron at the other end of the bar.

"Oh, yes," the bartender said, "and I bet he'll be here when I leave."

"I saw him at the car show," Audra Sue said, including Little Bobby in the conversation, "he's some sort of an ad executive with some big firm in New York. He blew it, though, at the car show. Got laughed off the stage. I felt so sorry for him."

"What happened?" Little Bobby asked.

Audra Sue gave him a quick summary of Scolio night: she was there, free-grazing the buffet, lights down, music up, little rat car unveiled, name was a little too close to reality. "And nobody who likes a woman dressed like this could be very big on reality." She told Little Bobby how the evening had ended. The ad man had slunk off like a dog who'd dirtied the rug.

"People can be so cruel," Audra Sue said. "It's such a gift, you know, to be creative, to come up with new thoughts, new ideas, and then there's always someone there to shoot you down."

Little Bobby was nodding, staring at the ad man, listening to the truth from Audra Sue.

The bartender set a drink on Audra Sue's tray. "If you're such a fan," the bartender challenged Audra Sue, "take him a fresh drink and let him cry on those milky white shoulders of yours."

Little Bobby grabbed the drink and headed toward the stranger.

# Chapter Twelve

Spike and Oxxie sat in a 50's style soda shop sipping chocolate malteds and eating large-cut fries, his ribbons from the parking lot on the seat next to Oxxie.

"The way I see it," Spike said, "we got three options. It's sort of a . . . a . . . uh . . ."

"Triage," Oxxie offered.

"No. Not a triage. That's like relating to emergency medical care."

"Yeah," Oxxie said.

"Here's the way I see it," Spike said, impatient with his straw, picking up the malted and leaving a brown mustache on his upper lip, "first, we could just go back to Mikey and tell him the truth—that we lost the chips and it's not our fault."

"Yeah. And then go to the triage," Oxxie said, dipping a french fry into his malted and guiding it carefully into his mouth. "What's our other choices?"

"Second, we could go back to Mikey and tell him we might be wrong about the description. Some guy jumps out of a car and points a piece, no one's gonna be counting his scars."

"Or his ears," Oxxie added.

"We tell him we might have made a mistake," Spike said. "That the case deserves, you know, further investigation. Might have been his brother in law— might not have been. We don't want a mix up on something as important as a right arm."

"Hmmm," Oxxie said. "Does your third alternative start with 'we go back to Mikey?'"

"No. Third, we go get the brother in law, kill him so he can never deny he took the chips, and take his arm to Mikey." Spike waved at the waitress for another malted.

"OH!" Oxxie said, grabbing his forehead with a massive hand that moved with the grace of a separate creature.

"What?"

"Brain freeze," Oxxie explained. "Have you ever killed anybody?" Oxxie asked, recovering.

"Sure," Spike answered, then, "you mean intentionally? No, I don't think so."

"You'd know. I have a thought."

"If you're asking whether I could kill Mikey's brother in law the answer's yes."

"See, I have a problem with that," Oxxie said, dipping two fries into the chocolate, constructing an edible airplane, and flying it into his mouth.

Spike leaned toward Oxxie and spoke softly, "If you have a problem with killing, you shouldn't even be in this business!"

"What business, Spike? All we've done so far is buy some casino chips," Oxxie reminded him. "That's not exactly death-defying."

"It's, uh, criminal enterprise. You get involved in a criminal enterprise and there's a chance some bodies might roll out." He cut his eyes toward the nearest booth. Two ten year olds were sharing a hot fudge sundae. "If you got moral qualms you should of never got involved."

"It's not that I got moral qualms, Spike. I just don't want to kill some gangster for some heist we made up and then have the whole organization and probably the cops down on us when Mikey finds out the truth."

Spike set his malt down and turned his head toward the window. "So, what do you think we should do?"

"Kill Mikey," Oxxie said. "He's our problem."

"I thought you didn't want to go back to Mikey."

"Not if he sees us coming."

# Chapter Thirteen

"Ms. Sharp," Detective Finch said, sitting on the couch while Berta Mae took the loveseat, "you may be the most marrying person I know."

"Why do you say that?" Berta Mae asked. She was an average size woman of probably 40, 45, with died black hair that went up like a crown roast on the top of her head and then fell back down in ringlets. Seemingly not unattractive under a layer of makeup, curvy eyeliner, and random beauty marks, her startling assets were her breasts. She looked like a referee carrying two basketballs chest high onto the court. She reeked of cigarette smoke with the faint tang of marijuana. She seemed quite mellow and a lot more cooperative than Finch had anticipated at the door.

"I ran your social security number on the way over here and it appears that you've been married twenty two times."

"Just a hopeless romantic, I guess," she smiled insincerely and somehow lifted and dropped her huge chest in a sigh.

"Mind if I ask how many are deceased?"

Berta Mae did some invisible math with her eyes on the small apartment's ceiling. "I really don't know," she finally said.

"Let me rephrase that question. How many died during the marriage?"

"Four," Berta Mae said, without having to hesitate. "My sweet Alex was the fifth," she added.

"Well, let's talk about him, first. How did y'all meet?"

"Detective, don't insult my intelligence. Why don't we just get to the point? I know why you're here."

"And why is that, Berta Mae? Is it alright if I call you Berta Mae?"

"You're here because Alex is dead and you think I had something to do with it."

"Well, I guess that's mostly true," Detective Finch said.

"Did that horrible Victor Marcuso send you?" Berta Mae asked.

"How do you know Victor Marcuso? You weren't ever married to him were you?"

"No, thank God. I worked there, but it's a long story," Berta Mae said.

"Bore me."

"Two to three years ago my then current husband played trumpet for their live show and he got me a job in the chorus line. I may not look it, Detective, but I was quite a dancer back east before I got dragged out to Vegas and dumped for a cocktail waitress."

"You danced on Broadway?" Finch asked.

"Close to it. I had an act with an albino python. Anyway, Davey, I think that was his name, the trumpet player, he got me a job in the chorus line and Victor Marcuso walked in the very first night, spotted me, and had me fired. Said I 'unbalanced' the line or something. Truth is, I put all the other girls to shame. You may not believe this, Detective, but" gesturing toward her bosom, "these puppies are for real."

"Ahemmm. So, you worked at the Four Winds, left there, have you worked anywhere else?"

"You mean dancing?"

"I mean anything. What do you do to pay the rent?"

"Oh. I don't pay rent. This place is mine. I inherited it. The antique shop downstairs pays rent to me."

"You inherited this place from a husband?"

Berta Mae nodded. "Eli. Dropped dead one day climbing the stairs."

Detective Finch made a mental note that they might want to exhume the body. "You must have inherited quite a lot. Do you have other property?"

"Real estate? No. Most of my husbands had a Will before we ever met," she said, a bit wistfully.

"Look, Berta Mae, we're probably going to eventually have to go over every one of your marriages, but right now I want to know about Alex Sharp."

Her features tightened. "You're going to make it look like I'm some kind of black widow."

"Not, necessarily," Finch said.

"You certainly are. You think I killed Alex."

"Frankly, Berta Mae, I don't see how."

"Well, I didn't."

"Tell me how you all met."

Berta Mae leaned back and her eyes danced around the apartment. If Finch were a poker player, which he was, he was bracing for a lie. "We met at one of the casinos on the Strip. I walked in, saw Alex standing there in those cute little safari shorts, we shared an all-you-can-eat buffet, and the rest is history."

"Uh huh. So, that was yesterday afternoon?"

"So much has happened since then."

"Which casino?"

"Uh, I think it was the Four Winds. I'm pretty sure it was."

"Well, I'm sure the meeting will be on tape, then," Finch said.

Berta Mae's painted eyebrows raised slightly as she nodded.

"And that was the first time you ever met Alex? Didn't know him before that?"

"Love at first sight," Berta Mae said.

"What did you do then? After the buffet."

Berta Mae gave Finch her best little coy look.

"You must have had sex if you're claiming you're pregnant."

Her eyes narrowed. "We had sex, Detective Finch. And I'm not just claiming I'm pregnant."

"Have you been to a doctor? Done one of those little EPT's?"

"No."

"But you're pregnant."

Berta Mae nodded. "A woman knows when she's pregnant, Detective." She touched her stomach. "I have life in me."

Finch massaged his right temple. "So, you got married. Whose idea was that?"

"Alex actually got down on his knees and proposed to me like a real gentleman. When I finally got him back to his feet, oh! That sounds cold. I didn't mean it like that."

"That's OK. Go on. What did you do when you got him erect?" If a man as black as Finch could blush, he was doing it. "You know what I mean. The bottom line is you guys got married."

"Of course."

"And then you went back out on the town?"

"Sure. I wanted to go back to the room but Alex said, let's have some fun: ride a roller coaster, watch the pirate show, go off the bungee tower."

"Did you promise him anything?"

"What do you mean?"

"Did you tell him you'd do anything for him if he went off the bungee tower?"

"We were married, Detective Finch. He could get anything he wanted from me at any time."

"Sure." Finch couldn't keep from smiling. "You've only been married for short periods. Why didn't you go off the tower with him?"

"He went off first and I watched. I didn't get a chance to do it. The cord broke, but you know all that."

"Did you say anything to him just before he jumped?"

"You mean before he got on the elevator? I told him I loved him."

"No, later, after he was on the tower. Did you shout anything up?"

"No, Detective, my last words to him were 'I love you.'" Berta Mae reached for a tissue on the coffee table, next to the closed laptop.

"Berta Mae," Finch said, standing smoothing his slacks. "We will meet again. Is there anything you've told me here today you need to change?"

"What do you mean?"

Finch smiled. "You know the routine, Ms. Sharp, as well as I do. You're not under oath, but you know it's a crime to lie to a police officer."

"Why would I lie?"

"And I don't recommend you leave town, either, until this whole thing is resolved."

"Detective Finch," Berta Mae said. "You really are a big man. Can I ask a personal question?"

Finch responded with a tentative, "Maybe."

"Did I hear you say you're married?"

# Chapter Fourteen

J. C. Martin barely raised his head when Little Bobby sat down beside him and put the drink on the bar, saying, "Howya doin', man?"

"You eber notish," J. C. said, staring at the same five cards on the video screen for the last three hours, head bobbing like a dashboard toy, eyes half closed, "how the nummers in the corner doan alwaysh mash the nummer of spotsh?"

"That's, uh, a ripoff," Little Bobby ventured.

"Yeah, a rib . . . a ripoff. Losh of riboffs in thish playsh. Losh Vegas is the land of riboff," J. C. said, raising a limp finger for emphasis.

J. C. suddenly leaned across the bar like a proctology patient. He twisted his neck to see Bobby. "Am I sposh to know you?" he said, eyes trying to focus.

Little Bobby's own eyes fluttered behind his lids. He stuck out his right hand for a shake and said, "Bobby Crest," but J. C. was unwilling or unable to take the hand so Bobby turned it into a shoulder pat.

"My wife diddun shent you here, did she? Sherve me with shomethin'?" J. C. sounded like a lost little boy.

"No no. I just saw you here and . . ."

"There's not much elsh to take. Can't cash a sheck or ush my plashtik. She even took my firsh clash ticket. Shecked me out of the hotel. Homelesh, joblesh, wifelesh, I got the cloesh on my bax."

"You got what?" Little Bobby asked. "The *cloesh*?"

"The cloesh. The *cloesh*. The cloesh on my *bax*. My bad."

The bartender stepped over. "The clothes on his back. I'm a certified interpreter for the drunk."

"There's a school for that?"

"Yeah. You're sittin' in it. Folks drink in the casino where they gamble. When they come in here they're usually busted and just trying to get drunk."

Little Bobby nodded and turned back to J. C. "You're an ad guy?" he said.

"Yesh one of the besh."

A guy in a Southern Baptist Convention tee shirt sat down at one of the bar tables with a lost-my-entire-retirement-account-on-red look and waved for bartender assistance. Audra Sue was nowhere in sight, probably in the bathroom trying to stretch her costume. The bartender leaned over and said to Little Bobby, "Call me over if you need me," and hurried off, a paramedic to an accident.

"You do, what, T.V. commercials, that sort of thing?" Little Bobby asked J. C.

J. C. pursed his lips and waved his hands in the air like swatting bees. "Evershang. Ever damn shang. Whole ad shampaigns. For shoap and shelebrities and shaports shars. Evershang."

Little Bobby called down to the bartender who was creating a very tall Long Island Tea for the baptist, "Shaports shars?"

"Sports stars," the bartender responded back over his shoulder, while sticking a lemon wedge on the rim of the glass and floating a cherry on top.

"Oh. Like an agent?" Little Bobby asked J. C.

"Not like agensh," he shook his head, almost tossing himself off the stool. "Like publishity. You know, like the logosh and tickish shales and evershang."

Little Bobby nodded a maybe. "Like, to create an image for the team, promote it. Make people want to get out of their living rooms for a live game."

"Maybesh. Defunutely maybesh."

"You might say that I, too, dabble in the sports industry." The Big Bobby in Little Bobby believed in luck and coincidences and grabbing opportunities. "Do you need a place to stay tonight?" Big Bobby would have asked, so Little Bobby did.

J. C. turned around on his stool to face Little Bobby. "Yoush one of thosh faggosh?"

Little Bobby called out to the bartender who was returning to refill the baptist's drink. "Faggosh?"

"No!" the bartender said. "Why does everyone ask? Is it my people skills or what I can do with my hands?"

"What?"

"The word is faggot, earmeister."

Little Bobby turned to J. C. "No, I'm not gay. I'm just offering you a place to sleep this off. Otherwise you may wind up out there on the Strip with tire tread on your face."

J. C. shut his eyes and considered his circumstances. Finally, he said, "I have noshing to pay you," a tear in his voice.

"Don't worry about it. Maybe we can bounce some ideas back and forth."

"Ideash? I'm loushy with ideas."

Little Bobby grabbed J. C. across the shoulders and started the long haul toward the front entrance.

"Come by more often," the bartender said. "You might find an accountant to carry home to do your taxes, or a lawyer to write your Will. It's like Purgatory. They all wind up here sooner or later, until somebody comes to get them."

Little Bobby shook his head and said to the bartender on the way out, "You're over-qualified."

# Chapter Fifteen

That night in the casino, Audra Sue was taking a drink order at a blackjack table and a familiar face looked up from his dwindling pile of chips, then quickly looked away.

"Hey," Audra Sue said, "aren't you Phil Riley?"

Riley kept his head down. "Are you talking to me?" he said.

"Phil Riley! Back in high school you worked at the marina on the lake and dated Cyndi Petray. You remember me? I'm Audra Sue." She mugged a smile and a cute little cock of her head.

Phil, head down, hand shielding his face, said, "I'm afraid you've made a mistake. It's been nice meeting you."

The dealer looked up at Audra Sue and shrugged.

Audra Sue started to speak, but closed her mouth tight, took the drink orders, and headed back to the bar. Halfway there, she heard a voice behind her.

"Audra Sue!" It was Phil Riley.

"Can we go someplace to talk?" Riley said.

She considered flipping the guy off, but that would not be Audra Sue. She sighed. "This is my last round on the tables," Audra Sue said, still a little skittish. "Meet me in the bar in ten minutes."

Audra Sue walked into the bar in a minute under ten, smiling, and Phil Riley was sitting at a video poker screen pouring in quarters like a submerged diver with a coin operated scuba tank. Riley didn't look up.

Audra Sue sat down, her smile fading. "What was all that?"

"What?" Riley mumbled a reply, attention riveted to the cards on the screen.

"The cold shoulder! You acted like you didn't even know me—like you were someone else," Audra Sue said.

"Wow. Look at that! I missed a royal straight by one card!" Riley said, dumping in another handful of quarters and pushing the button for another round.

"Are you just out here for the week, Phil?" Audra Sue asked.

"I saw someone hit $1200 on one of these things. I think the trick is to go after the royal flush every time."

"Do you still stay in touch with Cyndi?"

"But what's hard is when you already have a high pair. I'm not going to throw away two aces to go for a straight."

"The Martians just landed, Phil." Audra Sue warned. "And they're asking about you."

"Of course, then if you don't let go of the little cards you can never really hit the big hands."

When Phil Riley finally came up for a breath of real air, Audra Sue was gone.

# Chapter Sixteen

The desert sun streamed through Victor Marcuso's east window, decorating his office with silver splotches and sharp edged shadows. Marcuso poured two cups of steaming, aromatic coffee from a sterling pot.

"You take anything in your coffee, Detective?" Marcuso asked.

"Just black. Like me." Detective Finch said.

"You know, as crazy as the nights get around here, these bright desert mornings are becoming more and more welcome," Marcuso said, handing Finch a china cup with saucer and taking his seat behind the desk. "Nights of decadence, mornings of elegance. Who said that?" Marcuso already had his coat off, tie loosened, and sleeves rolled up. His mustache and goatee looked painted on, like that Russian guy, Finch thought, the guy with the statue.

"I don't know who said it," Finch said, sipping the coffee, "but it's gotta be about Vegas. At least the decadence part."

"I appreciate you keeping me updated on the investigation, Detective. I know that's not part of your job."

Finch nodded. "But the coffee's great, and I've got a few questions."

"Shoot," Marcuso offered, spreading his arms to allow a good shot.

"I found Ms. Sharp, a Berta Mae Pole, yesterday afternoon and we talked."

"What do you think?" Marcuso asked.

"Well, she's not a truthful person, I can tell you that. But she did say she knows you."

"Knows me?" Marcuso asked. "How does she know me?"

"The lady's had so many husbands I don't know what she called herself, but she was married to one of your musicians—a trumpet player named Davey. That name ring a bell?"

Marcuso shook his head. "Sorry. My orchestra leader might know him. How long ago was this?"

"I'll get more specifics when we interview her downtown, but she said it was two or three years ago. Apparently, Davey got her a job with the chorus line and you canned her."

"Now that could not have happened. I don't meddle with the live shows."

"She said you saw her in the chorus line and told the director that she was too well endowed, created a certain . . . imbalance in the line."

Marcuso got a sheepish grin on his face. "My god, I think I do remember that. I think I said there was a difference between sexy and just plain nasty. And you believe she's trying to get *even* for that?"

"I don't see how."

"How could she have known the cord would break?" Marcuso asked.

"My point exactly. I don't think she did know it would break. I do think she was *hoping* it would break, and the fact that you didn't have weight restrictions posted probably brought her to your place, instead of some revenge motive."

"We're going to get nailed on those weight restrictions, aren't we?"

"Time will tell. But I wouldn't think she'd be a very credible plaintiff. She took him there. She egged him on. And, she's got some history. I can't imagine a big verdict when the jury hears all that."

"History? You mean she's done this sort of thing before?"

"I think we'll discover that she's lost other husbands under suspicious circumstances, but we'll probably never prove she killed any of them. She may have exposed them to, even led them into, dangerous circumstances, but she may not have created the circumstances. We've got to show that she knew the circumstances would kill them—that she knew the cord would break."

"I'm not a cop or a lawyer," Marcuso said, "but I don't see how encouraging someone to take a bungee jump is enough for a murder indictment."

"I need to talk to the D. A., but, no, I don't think it is. You want to know what I think? I think she's running her own little perverted version of Make a Wish Foundation. We'll know more when we get her computer, but I bet she's working the internet to meet these guys who're already knocking on heaven's door. She gets them talking online about their health issues, then she lures the right ones here to Vegas, cuddles them with her charms, marries them if they're single and she can talk them into it, and then puts them in hazardous situations, hoping to hit the jackpot. Probably misses most of the time, but she keeps rolling the wheels for that fifty mil. The real jackpot is not just having the guy die, it's having him die under circumstances where someone else might be liable for his death."

Victor Marcuso raised a finger. "And that may be where Fitzlow Everhard comes in! Maybe they're conspiring on this thing."

"Maybe," Finch agreed.

"I'd love to see the Bar Association punch his ticket," Marcuso said, a sadistic grin on his face.

"It's all going to be hard to prove. We're going to have the computer picked up this morning on a search warrant. I have a mostly illegible copy of an email that Alex Sharp had in his pocket when he died, and I bet it'll turn out to be from Berta Mae. I'm convinced they didn't meet here, but they did make contact right here in your casino, and I'll need a copy of the surveillance tape from that afternoon."

"Done," Marcuso said.

"Tell your security guys to look for a woman with 36 Triple D's and a 500 pound guy in safari shorts," Finch said.

"Shouldn't be a huge problem," Marcuso said. "What about the pregnancy? Did you ask her about that?"

"Berta Mae said she hasn't been tested, but she said she's convinced. I say we'd better not put anything past her."

"What do you mean?"

"We just need to be ready for anything."

"You know," Marcuso said, filling his empty cup and holding the pot toward Finch, who declined, "I still feel like she's got us by the balls. I'd feel a lot better if she were looking at a murder rap," Marcuso said.

"Well, I would too. A lot of unsuspecting flies have flown into her web who didn't know it was a suicide mission. We're going to sweat her with what we get off her hard drive, but after she gets lawyered up the only way to nail her is to prove she knew the cord would break," Finch said, standing.

"How do we do that?"

"I don't know yet," Finch admitted, "but we need to get those specs and the lab results from the forensic lab."

"Will you keep me posted?"

"I will. Will you tell me something?" Finch asked.

"Sure."

"That line between sexy and just plain nasty. You ever need an outside opinion on that?"

# Chapter Seventeen

J. C. Martin's throat was ripped open from ear to ear by the fingernails of an evil witch with an uncanny resemblance to his wife and then she went after his privates as a hairy bearded elf by the name of Saul threw them both off a cloud cresting skyscraper. Judy was able to make a cackling escape on her broom toward the mall but J. C. fell and fell and fell until he fell face first into a shallow grave, surrounded by the relatives he shunned every Christmas. Smiling and singing Christmas carols they kicked dirt over him and then an army of Wall Street yuppies in three button suits with spiked haircuts and pointy noses marched over and over and over the grave until he woke up in Little Bobby's guest room, head splitting, bladder aching, and completely unaware of where or who he was. But the army kept marching. There were footsteps on the ceiling.

J. C. got out of bed by inching his legs off the side until his knees cleared the edge and his feet hit the floor, and then pushing himself upright with his arms. His head felt like it was as full of water as his bladder, a hard ocean sloshing against his skull, threatening to pour out his throat.

J. C. struggled upright like the first primate and took small and uncertain steps toward an open door, leading to a short hallway, presupposing a bathroom. He was so weak when he got there that he sat down to pee, but regretted sitting when he had to stand again. The tides were still changing inside his head, with a few ten foot waves thrown in for bad balance. Passing the mirror, careful not to look, J. C. stepped back into the hall, where a set of pull-down stairs connected to a hole in the ceiling.

He said in a voice loud enough for anyone in the house to hear, "Anyone want to tell me where I am?"

An upside down head popped out of the hole, further complicating J. C.'s equilibrium issues. "I'm Bobby Crest," it said, eyes closed and eyeballs fluttering behind the lids. "You came home with me last night to sleep it off. There's some coffee in the kitchen."

"To hell with coffee. I need some nourishment. Do you have any single malt scotch?"

"In the cabinet over the sink."

Dinosaur feet clumped toward the kitchen. A cabinet door creaked open. A lid clattered into the sink. A glug, glug happened. A few minutes later, J. C.

appeared at the bottom of the attic stairs, bottle in hand, throwing oil on the waters—twenty one year old oil. "I don't mean to sound unappreciative," he said, in a voice that sounded like pouring gravel into a pan, "but why have you been walking across my grave all morning?"

The upside down head appeared, eyes closed. "I'm looking for something." It disappeared.

"And I'm in hell," J. C. said, slumping backward down the wall to sit on the hall floor.

Minutes passed, J. C. sitting there, staring at the attic hole. Finally, J. C. took a solid pull on the scotch bottle, uttered an evil adjective, got up and started up the stairs. "Maybe I can help you look," he said.

"Watch out for the spiders," Little Bobby called out. J. C. stopped for another long pull on the bottle.

# Chapter Eighteen

Spike piloted the rental across a stark and lifeless desert plain. "It's the damn moon without craters," he said.

"The craters are up closer to Scary Larry's, where he tests his plastique," Oxxie said.

"Tell me what you know about this Scary Larry."

"He's an arms dealer," Oxxie said.

"Got that, but what do you know about him?"

"He's the head of a California-Nevada biker gang that goes by the name of Boom. Just, Boom."

"How many members?" Spike asked.

"One. Scary Larry. That, alone, should prove how scary he is."

"How did you meet him?" Spike asked.

"At the dentist office," Oxxie said.

"Scary Larry goes to the dentist?"

"To establish some records in the unlikely event of his demise," Oxxie said. "Actually, there's a rumor Scary Larry used to be a dental hygienist. That's how he got his name."

"The Scary part?" Spike asked.

"Yeah," Oxxie nodded. "Male hygienists take a lot of abuse, plus I understand he was a little obsessive-compulsive with his cleaning procedures. You know those crooked metal picks they use?"

Spike placed a hand on his jaw. "I really don't want to hear this. How much further is this place?"

"Go past that next dune and turn right," Oxxie said, pointing through a sand streaked windshield.

"See, now, that's the problem with you Oxxie; why I've learned to question your directions. Dunes move around. Haven't you ever heard of *shifting sand*? Hills stay in one place; dunes move around."

Oxxie nodded and pointed through the sand streaked windshield. "Go past that next hill and turn right."

The right turn revealed a low-slung shack, so airblasted by the sand that its walls were curved. Sitting in front of the house was a Nevada Highway Patrol motorcycle.

"Uh oh," Spike said.

"It's OK. Scary Larry also deals in used motorcycle parts. Every time a Highway Patrol bike goes missing, they put out another APB on Larry."

A wooden, three foot fence surrounded the property, creating a square with the curvy house in the center. "What's up with the short fence?" Spike said. "Is Scary Larry a damn midget?"

"I'd keep your voice down on that issue, Spike. Scary Larry went down once for illicit midget wrestling, turned out to be twelve year olds, but we don't want to go there. There's another reason for the low fence. A jump attack."

"Jump attack?" Spike hopped out of the car and strode straight up to the fence. Oxxie followed, a safe distance behind.

Spike put his hands to his mouth, megaphone style, and shouted, "Anybody home? Scary Larry! You home?"

Oxxie braced himself. "You gotta learn everything the hard way, dontja Spike?"

From around the corner of the house came a blur of legs and teeth and slobber with a ground speed of at least 100 miles an hour. Before Spike could breathe or turn or even wet his pants, the Doberman hit its mark a few feet on the other side of the fence and was airborne, eyes wide, mouth open, teeth dripping, and emitting a deep guttural growl that could mean nothing but disaster. That horrible face flew over the short fence and at Spike at such a speed that Spike could only close his eyes in anticipation of impact.

And, he waited, for impact.

Finally Spike opened one eye, and the dog's toothy drooly growling face was there, inches from his own. And he shut his eye. It occurred to Spike that he might have slipped into some other dimension of time and space—time crawling by, just before his face was eaten, then a warm, wet, lathery thing touched him on his chin and moved up over his lips, up the bridge of his nose, across his eyelids, and up his forehead. He opened both eyes, and took a moment to pee down his leg.

Oxxie held the Doberman in both arms, tight against his chest, where he had snagged it in mid-leap, business end still aimed at Spike's face. Oxxie was rubbing his face on the dog's black fur saying, "Honeypie just came out to say hello, didn't little Honeypie? How's my sweet Honeypie?" The Doberman cooed.

"You know the dog?" Spike managed to ask, two octaves higher than usual.

"Met him at the dentist office. I took her out back while Scary had his x-rays. Shows the value of regular dental checkups."

"Let's get this thing over with," Spike said, stepping out of the puddle he'd created and placing his hands to his mouth once again.

"Don't yell for Scary Larry," Oxxie said. "He sees us. He'll be out when he's ready."

On those words, the door of the shack slammed open, slammed shut, and then slammed open again. Oxxie put Honeypie back in the yard, where she tucked her tail and slunk away from the shadow on the porch.

"May I ga'damn help you gentlemen?" It wasn't a booming voice, but it certainly filled the void. It was a well modulated tone, like a radio guy. In fact, the shadow on the porch looked like that tall radio guy with the long hair.

Spike started to speak but Oxxie gently pushed him back. "Scary, it's Oxxie."

"Yes, I ga'damn see that. I look out my ga'damn window, I say, well, Scary, that's either Oxxie Bozone or the ga'damn Big Foot."

"You refer to yourself in private as Scary?" Spike asked.

"Ga'damn. Who's your ga'damn friend with the wet leg, Oxxie?"

"This is Spike, Scary, and he's OK," Oxxie said. "We're here to find some hard to find stuff, Scary."

"What do you need to ga'damn do with that hard to find stuff?" Scary asked, taking a little ring binder and the stub of a pencil from his shirt pocket; licking the pencil lead. "You need something on the national or international level, or is this more in the ga'damn private sector?"

"Private, Scary. We need to make a bad guy disappear."

Scary made some marks on his notepad. "A bad guy. Completely disappear, or just be ga'damn hard to piece together?"

"Completely. Do a Hoffa."

Scary made some marks on his notepad. "You want it to ga'damn hurt, or just be quick and sudden?"

Oxxie looked at Spike and they both shrugged at one another. "Probably just be quick, Scary, and easy," Oxxie said.

Scary made more marks on the notepad. "Will this ga'damn happen in close quarters or out in the open?"

Oxxie said, "Let's go for close quarters on that one, Scary."

Scary Larry said, "Hmmmm" closed the notepad and went into the shack. Honeypie came over to the fence and jumped up on Oxxie and Oxxie scratched her behind the ears. The dog ducked away when Scary walked out of the house with a brown paper bag, gesturing for Oxxie to come get it. Oxxie stepped over the fence and retrieved the bag from Scary, exchanging a handful of cash on the porch. Scary said "Have a nice day," and went back in and closed the door behind him.

When Spike and Oxxie were back in the car, Spike said, "I didn't hear a price mentioned. How did you know how much to give him?"

"I wasn't sure. I just guessed. If it's more he'll come see us."

"Ga'damn," Spike said, louvering the air conditioner vent to blow on his wet crotch. "Lemme see in the bag!"

Oxxie held the bag tight to his chest. "My mother always said, 'don't open your toys until you're home.'"

# Chapter Nineteen

The attic, well lit as attics go, was lined on each side and part of the middle with metal filing cabinets, half of which had been opened and their contents stacked on top or piled on the plywood floor.

"What's all this?" J. C. asked, placing the scotch bottle on the attic floor.

"These are the fossilized remains," Little Bobby said, not looking up from a file he was flipping through, "of my dad's fifty years in the hotel and casino distribution business."

"A lot of paper," J. C. said.

"Back when everything was on paper. And he never threw anything away."

"What are you looking for?"

Little Bobby stopped and turned to J. C. "I get a call from Victor Marcuso yesterday and he wants to see me. Says their damn bungee cord broke that they bought from my dad several years ago and they want whatever paperwork we might have on it. Says I could get sued and lose the house."

J. C. whistled. "Serious." J. C., a man who'd always had a very efficient secretarial staff, gestured toward the filing cabinets. "Why don't you just go to the Four Winds file and look under 'B,' for bungee cord?"

"My dad had a system," Little Bobby said, "wherever there was a space in a file drawer, that's where he'd file something, irregardless of customer, description or date. I've got to go through every one of these drawers until I find it."

"Well, I can help." J. C. said, certain that the scotch couldn't get any better on the street.

"I'd appreciate that," Little Bobby said. "If you want to you can start on that other end. Look for invoices to the Four Winds, any old product catalogs, I'd say for the last six to seven years, and anything on bungee cords. Just set it all apart and we'll go through it together."

J. C. stepped over to a file cabinet and slid it open. Dust billowed into his face and a grey legged spider scampered out of the light. He went back to retrieve the bottle.

It took J. C. a while to figure out what he was looking for, but, within the hour, he was nearing Little Bobby's speed in opening, perusing and discarding files. As the late morning sun began to heat the roof, Little Bobby said, "I'm going downstairs to order us a pizza."

J. C.'s stomach gurgled an affirmative reply. "See if they'll bring beer," J. C. said. J. C. stopped and turned toward Little Bobby, "I'm going to pay you back for all this Bobby. J. C. bounces back."

Little Bobby waved and climbed down the stairs to call for the pizza. By the time he'd gotten back up, J. C. was holding a file folder in his hand.

"Did you find something?" Little Bobby asked.

"I want you to look at this," J. C. said. "It's an electrical schematic for a poker table at the Four Winds."

"It's not a poker table that we're . . ."

"No no, Bobby, look at this. Ask yourself, 'what is electrical about a poker table?'"

Little Bobby shared his attention between the schematic and J. C.'s questioning stare. "I don't get it," Little Bobby finally said.

"Well, I have some suspicions," J. C. said.

By the time the pizza arrived, Little Bobby and J. C. were sitting at the dining room table, twisting and turning the schematic, trying to read its small print and to understand its circuitry.

J. C. put his finger on one point. "This," he said, "is a camera with an attached transmitter. That was really cutting edge stuff back then—four, five years ago. You've got nine pinhole cameras, built into the edge of the table with a potential view of the players' hole cards. Each has, see those little numbers? Each has a frequency recorded right on the schematic."

"What we're looking at," Little Bobby said, "is probably one of those tournament tables, where the hole cards are broadcast on T.V."

"No. And I'll tell you why. Why would each camera have its own frequency? If they were rigged for a T.V. broadcast they'd be hardwired and switched at a console. This is *covert* wiring, Bobby. *Covert.*"

"What are you suggesting?"

"I'm saying if you took a little T.V. in there and flipped through the UHF frequencies, you would eventually connect to one of these wireless cameras. Depending on the remote range, you could get a picture anywhere in the casino; maybe further."

"How do we know these tables are still in use?"

"Easy way to find out. Let's just take a little hand held T.V. in there and run through the frequencies. Tell me something, Bobby. Was your dad a really good poker player? Seem to always know what the other guy had?"

"Yeah," Little Bobby said. "He had a reputation for that."

J. C. nodded, his Wall Street mind beginning to smoke. He took a large bite of pepperoni pizza, saving the beer for later. "We may be able to do that, too."

"Look, J. C., I hate to throw a damper on all this, but I'm busted. I don't have ten cents in the bank and it was a miracle that pizza would fit on my credit card. Now you're talking about hand held T.V.'s and . . ."

"Okay. I know. I'm sorry. I'm not contributing much here. I've still got a few friends in New York who ought to wire me a few thousand. I'll check on that. If we find the right buyer we may even want to sell this schematic, but we can't do that unless we check it out, see if it's real. See if the table is still in use."

Little Bobby said, "You say any T.V. ought to pick up the signals if it's tuned to the right frequency?"

"Should."

"I've got an idea that might save us the price of a new set."

# Chapter Twenty

Spike "the Word" Spivey was whirling like a Dervish.

"What is a Dervish?" Oxxie asked.

"It's sort of an evangelical Muslim," Spike said, jumping on a scale outside a health food store but hopping back off before it had time to register a weight. "Known for wild rituals."

"You're whirling like one," Oxxie said.

Mikey "Don't Call Me Cheeso" Mozzarelli circled behind the carousel and stopped to survey the international offerings at the food court. Spike and Oxxie ducked inside a Starbucks. Mikey seemed to decide on a particular nation for lunch and got in a short line. Spike and Oxxie circled around the outside perimeter of the tables. Mikey turned, glancing in their general direction. They darted inside another Starbucks.

"Do you think he's on to us?" Spike asked Oxxie. Oxxie followed Spike, single file, out into the mall to a tall clump of artificial palms, where they stood in a vertical line behind a paper mache trunk.

"If he was on to us he'd come over and shoot us, Spike."

Spike pulled out a spiral pad, much like Scary Larry's, except it had happy faces on it, and jotted notes. "So, his routine for today was to take Mrs. Mikey to the salon at Neimans. He's lucky she's with him. Otherwise, we could blow him up when he leaves the mall."

"I'm not sure we should be crawling under his car in a public lot—in broad daylight," Oxxie said.

"Well, he'd spot us in his own driveway. What do you suggest?" Spike asked.

"At least we do it in the dark," Oxxie said. "He doesn't take his wife to that whorehouse near his place."

"Why should he? Lookout!" Spike said, flattening himself in the plastic bushes. A woman in a short red skirt said "pervert" as she walked by. "He's got his food and he's headed for the tables!" Spike said.

Mikey took a small tray to a short line of booths, still some distance from Spike and Oxxie, but certainly within eyeshot, if not gunshot.

"We're not going to do anything here but get caught," Spike said. "Let's regroup back at the car." Oxxie agreed.

When Spike and Oxxie exited the mall, wails of sirens and the flashing lights of emergency vehicles greeted them.

"Wow," Spike said, "I wonder what happened. Look at that black smoke."

As they drew closer to where they had parked the rental, they saw a group of firemen hosing down a hump of smoking metal.

"You left the bag in the car, didn't you?" Oxxie asked.

"I wasn't going to walk around the mall with a bag in my hand," Spike said.

"Yeah. Bags at malls are pretty suspicious. I guess this settles an earlier argument we had," Oxxie said.

"What's that?"

"Heat *can* make it blow up."

Later, Spike and Oxxie parked their new rental outside Scary Larry's.

"I'll wait in the car," Spike said.

Oxxie nodded. "Good idea." He got out and was gone for ten minutes, while Spike drummed an entire John Williams soundtrack on the steering wheel.

When Oxxie got back, smelling like a Doberman, Spike said, wiggling his fingers in the air, "What did big ol' hairy Scary Larry say?"

"You don't want to know."

"If I didn't want to know I wouldn't ask," Spike said.

"He said, 'Ga'damn. That little prick cause a premature explosion?'"

Spike screwed up his face and gripped the wheel. "Maybe we ought to blow him up when we finish with Mikey."

"Yeah. By then we be experts."

# Chapter Twenty One

Detective Finch tapped on the edge of Shauna Tell's open door, and she looked up from a law review article she seemed to be committing to memory. She flipped the book into the pile on her desk.

"Well lawsy mercy wouldja just look at who security let through!" Shauna put her hands on her generous hips as she stood. "In this corner, at six feet, one hundred and something pounds, in the blue suit, you got a mean black woman who's been stood up for lunch. Ya wanna fight?"

"Sorry, Shauna. We had an emergency. Car blew up at the mall."

"Anybody in it?"

"No."

"Then it wasn't an emergency. Good riddance, I'd say." Shauna flashed her record breaking smile. "Don't make me have to bend you over this desk, Harry."

Harrison Finch glanced up and down the hall of the District Attorney's office, convincing himself that everyone had heard that last comment. He stepped into Shauna Tell's office and shut the door, taking a seat in an old wooden chair that visibly wobbled with his size.

"On the other hand, Harry, maybe you need to miss a few lunches. Looking a little thick in the gut." Shauna Tell was the pride of the District Attorney's office. Every year for twenty years she had turned down lucrative private practice offers to continue prosecuting murders and mayhem for the county, making clear to any poor, unfortunate defendant who might wander into her courtroom, "You see what Charles Barkley can do with that ball? It's nothing compared to what I'm gonna do to you, brother." And, then she did. She'd racked up some impressive numbers, especially in child abuse cases, and kept the photos of the children she'd battled for pinned to her office wall.

"I'm sorry about lunch, Shauna. I really needed to talk to you about a case I'm working."

"Since when did you start letting the law get tangled up with your investigations?"

"Well, this one's a few degrees off center. Did you hear about that bungee death at the Four Winds?"

"I did. You think it was a homicide?" Shauna leaned forward across her desk as far as her upper bulk and her crowded desk would allow. "I heard that some fatty jumped off and the cord broke."

"You ever run across a woman named Berta Mae Pole?"

"Name doesn't sound familiar," Shauna said.

"I haven't run all her aliases, and she has a few. Married over twenty times."

"Good god!" Shauna said, "More rings than the giant sequoias! And you and I worry about two divorces between us! Maybe we ought to give it another go, big Harry, if it's as easy as all that!"

Finch ignored Shauna's weekly marriage proposals. "My guess is, she meets up with guys on the internet. Guys with health problems. Then she . . ."

"Makes them go bungee jumping."

"Yeah, among other things."

"I dunno," Shauna said. "I see what you're saying. She rides them hard and puts them up wet. Which is fine, probably quite fine for them, until one day they don't come back from the ride."

"You're quick. Do you see an indictment in all of that?"

"You can show it's a pattern; not just the one thing the other night?"

"She's had other husbands die. We're checking that. I think we'll see a pattern."

"What about her computer? Does she have a web site or anything?"

"We got her computer this morning on a warrant, but all the files and half the hard drive was erased," Finch said, cursing himself for not getting it before he confronted her.

"Well, that proves something right there, and you know what our techies say. You can erase the files, but unless you take out the hard drive and burn it and then take a shotgun to the internet provider, you'll never really get rid of them. We can restore them."

"I hope so."

"Is she lawyered up, yet?"Shauna asked.

"She's got Fitzlow Everhard as her civil attorney suing the Four Winds. I don't know if he'd handle a criminal case."

Shauna shook her head. "Fitzlow Everhard. That old duck. He'd handle a porcupine for a fee."

"Victor Marcuso said we might look into a conspiracy between the two."

"How so?"

"Fitzlow advises Berta Mae how to construct a personal injury lawsuit; she fits the pieces together."

Shauna nodded, a twinkle in her eye. "Maybe I could speak with Fitzlow," she said, "maybe put the fear of God in him?"

"Do it. I'll keep working on the computer angle. And I'm going to check out the other dead husbands. Shauna," Finch said, "I really want to see us make a case here."

"If there's a case here we'll make it. We're good, Harry. If not, you'll probably make the case anyway and I'll turn it down. Why are you so adamant on this one, Harry? Did Berta Mae punch your buttons?"

"Honestly?"

"Might be nice for a change."

"I feel sorry for these guys. It's bad enough to be knocking on heaven's door—think how they feel when someone opens the door and kicks them through."

"And?"

"And what?" Finch said.

"Why else? You've worked a thousand murders, Harry. Don't tell me you didn't feel sorry for every one of those stiffs."

"Okay. But this is just a small part of my motivation, you understand. And *your* murder will be my next investigation if you tell anyone."

"Speak to me, Harry!"

Finch kicked his right shoe with his left as he talked. "I want to work for the Four Winds. You know, one of the casinos. I've looked at as many mangled corpses as anyone should ever have to see. I've been shot at, suckerpunched, investigated by IA, and forced to see a shrink. I've got a little retirement check I can draw, a daughter who doesn't need any more tuition, and a pretty good reputation if I don't deck someone before I quit. I want to sit in an office and tell guys how to bust cheaters or even walk the floor myself. I'll stand guard over their whales. I don't care. I don't want to suck up to any more judges or be on the losing end of a killer gone free or a child rapist with enough money for a good lawyer. I just don't want to do it anymore, and I can make more money and work less hours at a casino."

"Wow," Shauna said. "And this case could do that?"

"Maybe. If I do it right."

"Do it right, Harry. You know what I mean? Do it exactly right."

"I know what you mean. That's why I'm here," Finch said.

"And when you get that great, cushy job . . ."

"Yeah?"

"Take me with you."

"You still hungry?" Finch asked.

"Is that a proposal?" Shauna asked.

"Maybe I could just have a salad."

# Chapter Twenty Two

"So what's your name?" Little Bobby asked the bartender, his eyes almost shut, some activity at the slits. "I never did get your name last night."

"I'm the bartender. That's not capitalized. There are too many names in this world already." Speaking to J. C., "You look a little better."

"I can't say I feel a lot better," J. C. said.

During the busy time of the evening, the bar served a section of six blackjack tables with one or two waitresses alternating through with trays. In the early afternoon, that section was closed. The bartender polished glasses, checked the level of his soft drink tanks, and spent a lot of time leaning and waiting for the evening rush. "What're you guys drinking?"

"Nothing right now," J. C. said, "but, could we ask a favor?"

"You can ask."

"Could we have the remote to the T.V.?" Little Bobby said, gesturing toward a small set built right into the far end of the counter alongside the video poker screens. A silent weather report crawled across a pastel background.

"Sure," the bartender said. "Not much on. It's all closed circuit, but if you hurry you can catch a breathtaking review of our restaurants and live shows."

"That's the other thing," Little Bobby said, his eyes doing that thing again. "Could we get you to disconnect the cable?"

The bartender frowned and bent under the counter. "Do you guys sit at home and plan how you're going to harass me?" The weather report disappeared. When the bartender arose, he handed the remote to Little Bobby. "If there's something you have to see on local T.V. I don't recommend this set. We get zero reception inside the casino."

"It'll be alright," J. C. said, his eyes already glued on the screen.

The bartender shook his head and walked down to the other end of the bar. The phone was ringing.

Little Bobby started a review of the stations beginning with channel 3 showing in the upper right corner of the set. When he got to 13, J. C. said, "Now we'll find it. We're getting into the UHF frequencies."

"What does UHF mean?" Little Bobby asked.

"You've got VHF and UHF. In broadcast classes we called them Very High Frequencies and Ungodly High Frequencies," J. C. answered. He laughed. "You know, this may be the first time in ten years I've been able to use my ivy league degree."

When the displayed number was in the mid-forties, Little Bobby hesitated, his thumb wearing out. "Doesn't look good," he said.

"Give me the clicker," J. C. said. He took the remote from Little Bobby's hand and began pushing it with his own bent thumb. Finally, at channel 76, a movement appeared through the white fuzz on the screen.

"Look," J. C. said, "did you see that?"

"I see something."

"I wish this set had fine tuning." J. C. flipped to the next channel. Again, faint activity stirred behind the static.

"Flip it again," Little Bobby said.

J. C. did, and said, "Oh, my god! Look at that!"

Both men bent into the screen: a wide stretch of green, apparently felt, hands moved at the upper left, probably the dealer, cards flew into sight, face down, and then another set of hands, much nearer, turned up a pair of fives.

"Do you see that?" both men said in unison, eyes wide, breathing like they were peeping through their neighbor's window.

"*Now*," J. C. said, "all we have to do is figure out which table in the casino we're looking at."

"*Now*," the bartender said, placing two bottled beers on the counter, and leaning between them, eyebrows arched, "all you have to do is pick up these beers while I still have this ingenuous smile on my face and walk, don't run, out of this casino." He smiled an ingenuous smile.

"Why?" Little Bobby said, pushing the off button on the remote as the screen clicked black.

"You've been fersed. That was the phone call. Pick up and go, gentlemen."

They picked up and went.

"Fersed?" J. C. asked as they pushed through a side entrance and began the long, hot walk to Little Bobby's house, on a short side street between the airport and the Strip.

"I've read about it. It's been around since the big card counting teams from the east coast started hitting the casinos. It's a computerized surveillance system. They can take a still photo right off their VCR tapes or they can scan in a picture, and anytime their cameras detect that person in the casino a buzzer goes off in the surveillance room and the person's tracked by pursuit cameras. It's called something like Features Recognition System. FRS. We were FRSed. Fersed."

"So why would we be fersed? They couldn't know about the schematic."

"I bet Marcuso red-flagged me after I left his office yesterday. He probably thinks I know more about that bungee cord than I let on. He may think I'm in on the whole deal. Hell, I don't know. These people are just paranoid, and they love to play with their surveillance toys."

"If they only knew what we were doing in there," J. C. said. "Our own little surveillance toy."

"I hope that bartender plugged the cable back in," Little Bobby said.

J. C. stopped. "Did he see what was on the screen when he came over?"

"I don't know. Oh crap!" Little Bobby pointed down the street. A moving van was parked at the curb and men in orange overalls were hauling filing cabinets up its ramp with dollies. Little Bobby jogged to his front yard.

"What in the hell is going on?"

A uniformed officer stepped out of Little Bobby's front door, unfolding a set of papers. "Mr. Bobby Crest?"

"What is this? These guys look like county inmates. What are they doing in my house?" Little Bobby asked.

"I'm Sheriff Boyd, Mr. Crest. This here is a court order requiring that we secure all records belonging to the company CrestLine."

"This is crazy. These are my records. You went inside my house and searched my house with convicts and now you're taking these files?"

"It's all right here in the court order, Mr. Crest," Sheriff Boyd pointed a tobacco stained finger at the order. "I'm directed to do what the judge tells me to do. No one answered the door, so we entered. We didn't have to search the house because we had information that the records were in the attic."

"Marcuso," Little Bobby said with a hot blast of air. "No wonder the bastard didn't want me in his casino. Thought I might be there for a piece of him."

"You really need to take up any problem you have with the judge, Mr. Crest. If you continue to use profanity or in any way block our progress I may have to arrest you," the Sheriff said.

"You want to hear some profanity, Sheriff? You want to see some blocked progress?"

J. C. grabbed Little Bobby by the arm and corralled him toward the curb, a safe distance from the moving van. "Sit down," J. C. said, and Little Bobby reluctantly complied. They both sat, feet in the street.

"This is not right!" Little Bobby said, his face streaked with sweat and furrows of blood-red flush lines.

"I know it's not right. We'll sue the bastard. We'll own his god damned casino."

"I guess Marcuso thought I wasn't going to bring him the specs. I guess I didn't work fast enough for Mr. Victor Marcuso!"

"Bobby," J. C. said, his voice lower, strained, hand chopping the air for emphasis, "let me tell you my concern, okay? What's the chance of there being another schematic like the one I've got in my back pocket?" J. C. asked.

"What do you mean?"

"Somewhere in all those files, Bobby, there's going to be another schematic, maybe for another table or a table at another casino. Forget the files, Bobby. Let them look for the damn bungee cord. But, what if they find out about the table?"

"So?"

"So?" J. C. repeated. "We just found a treasure map, Bobby. We just found a way to turn it all around, and now you're going to let that go? They'll have every table in the place, maybe every table in Vegas, shut down and examined for cameras if they find one damn hint of what your dad was doing."

"Well, what do we do about it now? They've got the files." Bobby pointed a desperate finger toward the truck.

"Offer to go with the files. Make peace with the Sheriff and tell him you know your dad's organization system. Maybe you can find the schematics before they do."

"Slim chance," Little Bobby said.

"The only chance we've got," J. C. said.

Little Bobby got up from the curb and walked over to talk to the Sheriff.

"Sheriff Boyd," he said, "I can help you guys find what you need in these files."

"Good," Sheriff Boyd said, assisting a county prisoner to bump a file cabinet down the front steps.

"No. I mean, if you'll let me help, I can probably find what you need."

Sheriff Boyd turned and faced Little Bobby head-on. "You can take that up with Victor Marcuso, Mr. Crest. I've got instructions to deliver these files to the Four Winds this afternoon and after that it's out of my hands."

Little Bobby turned back to J. C. and shrugged. "Plan B?" Little Bobby asked.

"Plan B is, we've got to act fast," J. C. said.

At about that time, Victor Marcuso and Harrison Finch shared a telephone conversation.

"You got a judge to sign a court order for county personnel and work release inmates to break into his house and pick up his files. That's . . . uh . . . impressive, Mr. Marcuso."

"Well, Detective Finch, some members of the bench are not as discreet with their gaming habits as others. We have a few judges who'll take care of us as well as we take care of them."

"That sounds like a bribe," Finch said.

"Of course not. We give comps all the time, Detective, and no one calls them bribes. Not if they want them to continue. This is sort of a judicial comp. Do you have a problem with that?"

"None," said Finch, chewing on the word, clicking his phone shut.

"Who was that?" Shauna asked, sipping her sweetened tea.

"My future," Finch said.

# Chapter Twenty Three

Audra Sue leaned over the bartender and said, "Whatcha watchin'?"

Her voice lifted him a foot off the stool and he came down with his palms spread out over the screen. "Holy guacamole! You scared the shuck off of me!" The bartender fumbled for the remote and found the off button, but not before Audra Sue said, "Hey, what was that?"

"What?" the bartender said, "what was what?"

"On the T.V. The hand with the big Texas ring was turning up two Queens."

"Oh, that. One of those dumb celebrity poker tournaments," the bartender said, "I was looking for the ballgame." He stood, went behind the counter, and Audra Sue watched him busy himself slicing a lemon into a bowl overflowing with sliced lemon.

Audra Sue said, "Well, whatever. I start in about a minute and it looks like I'll be working this section again. Uh . . ."

"What?" the bartender asked, sticking a nicked thumb into his mouth.

"Nevermind." Audra Sue took a tray and whirled away into the casino.

The bartender shook his head and let out a stream of tepid air.

But, it wasn't over. When Audra Sue came back through with the first round of drink orders, she set the tray down and said, "I'm sorry about earlier."

"What do you mean?" the bartender said.

"The last time I saw a guy act like that was when I walked in on my little brother with the swimsuit issue."

"You just . . . startled me."

"Yeah, him too. Look, I circled around the blackjack tables and then checked out the poker pit. There's a man with that ring sitting at the high stakes table betting about ten thousand dollars a hand," Audra Sue said. "You were looking at his cards on the T.V. How can the casino get away with that?"

The bartender put a finger to his lips, and motioned Audra Sue behind the counter. He turned on a blast of water at the sink. His lips barely moved when he spoke. "The casino doesn't do that. You remember the two who were in here last night? They came in and tuned the T.V. to some channel and that's what came on."

"The ad guy and the guy with the funny eyes?"

"Them."

"Wow. They must have a camera out there. How do they do that?"

"I don't know, but the casino knows something because they don't want the little one in here. He was fersed."

"What?"

"They recognized him when he came in and I think security was on the way to the bar when he left," the bartender explained.

"You know," Audra Sue said, gesturing toward the T.V., "someone could make a lot of money with that."

"*Someone*, girl? *We* could," the bartender said.

"Us? How?" Audra Sue asked. "Oh my god! I see. We can tune in on the same camera."

"Or cameras," the bartender said. "I think we'd better find out what security knows."

Audra Sue sucked her lips into a thin line, then a smile reached all the way up to her eyes. "They can't know everything," she said.

"Why?"

"If they did, they'd go rip out that camera."

"You're right," the bartender said. "I think you're right. Whoever wins at those poker tables isn't winning the casino's money, but no casino would allow cheating if they could stop it. Even a rumor of something like that could close the doors. I don't think they know either. We need to sniff around and find out what they do know."

"So, we're in this together?" Audra Sue asked, eyes wide. "I'm not sure I can do anything illegal." Her eyes scanned the hatchings in the rubber matted floor, her arms crossed. "I've seen those movies and I don't think I'd do very well in one of those women's prisons."

"Me neither," the bartender said. "So let's not get caught."

"That's not what I mean," Audra Sue said.

"We didn't plant the cameras. I can't see a whole lot wrong with turning on a T.V. set and changing channels."

"Whatever," Audra Sue said, shaking it off with a glum shrug. "I guess we're in this together."

"Together," the bartender nodded, crowsfeet of concern at his eyes. They exchanged a discreet high five. "Now give me your drink orders before they fire us both—together."

# Chapter Twenty Four

Phillip Riley ran out of chips on split 8's, making two 18's while the dealer topped him with a 20. He reached in his pants pocket, already knowing he'd find nothing but lint and a couple of pawn tickets. Phil got up and left the table, the last bad-beat still clouding his vision, and found the elevator. On the way up to his room he bet himself there would be at least one stop. He lost. He stepped off the elevator on his floor, onto the long, empty, carpeted hall and he whispered "dead man walking," which was a dark joke he'd begun to tell himself on his more and more frequent visits to the small steel safe edged into the corner of his closet.

When he opened the door and stepped inside the room, the telephone rang, and, against his better judgment, he picked it up.

"Agent Riley?" the caller asked.

"Who is this?" he said.

"Assistant Executive Under Secretary of Personnel Milton McMix here. What time is it there in Las Vegas, Agent Riley?"

Phillip glanced at the white strip of skin around his left wrist. "I'm not sure," he said, wondering how McMix knew he'd pawned his watch.

"It's 1:23 here. 1:24. Agent Riley, I've left numerous messages."

Phillip said, "Sorry. I've been busy."

McMix growled. "Agent Riley I must tell you that I am very concerned. Very concerned indeed." Phillip could see McMix's fat jowls quaking. "Your voucher amounts total $65,000! That's for under forty days. I don't know what you've been so busy with, but, to date, not one report has been filed."

"Report?" Phillip said.

McMix growled louder. "You know, Agent Riley, *report*. As in, the reason you are there: evidence of criminal activity; the money-laundering that was supposed to be so prevalent. The task force says you've been out of touch with them since mid-month. And I don't think they're telling me everything."

"Sir, I've been on the job in the casino twenty hours a day."

"Well," McMix said, "something's not right. We're pulling you back. You're going to be reassigned under the special agent in charge there in Las Vegas, and then most likely transferred. I want you downtown in his office by tomorrow morning at 8:00. Is that understood? And I think you'd better start preparing a defense for those vouchers."

"I understand," Phil moaned, as the Washington connection ended.

"I should go to bed now," Phil said aloud, unbuttoning his shirt and heading for the shower, "I should call the desk, leave a wake-up call for 7:00, and go straight to bed." On the way to the shower, Riley paused by the hall closet where the room safe was riveted into a corner. He knelt, punched a few numbers on the pad and the door sprung open, revealing a lone stack of cash, still bound with a bank wrapper. He picked up the stack, folded it, and stuck it into his pants pocket, then he buttoned his shirt and left the room.

# Chapter Twenty Five

J. C. stayed on the phone most of the afternoon. Little Bobby had never seen a male talk on the phone so long or with so much animation. At a short breather, Little Bobby asked him how he could do it.

"I'm not great with power tools. I'd probably wreck an 18-wheeler the first time I backed it up. My writing skills could be better. But I do good phone. You can't earn a living on the eighteenth floor anywhere unless you do good phone."

Little Bobby stayed on the couch and alternated between listening to J. C.'s quick and persuasive patter, hearing the same jokes about nine times in as many different conversations, and fretting about the CrestLine records.

"Ok," J. C. finally put down the phone and clapped his hands together, "here's what I've got. In about an hour I can go down to the money transfer place and pick up a few thousand. That gives us a little walking around money. We can go from there to one of those little spy shops."

"Spy shops?" Little Bobby asked.

"Oh, you know, those places that sell concealed cameras and mace and what-not. We need a good, battery operated hand-held T.V. with a quick fine tuning adjustment. We also need, and here's the big one, a one-way communication system. You need to be able to talk to me through a virtually invisible earpiece while I'm sitting at the table."

"Talk to you?" Little Bobby asked.

"Tell me the cards. You can't go in there and play, Bobby. I'm going to have to play and you're going to have to be somewhere else."

Little Bobby wrinkled his forehead. "J. C.," Bobby started.

"And I called the casino. I asked whether they had any big poker tournaments coming up and they have a Sit & Go every Monday, Wednesday, and Friday at 9:00 a.m. Do you know what a Sit & Go is, Bobby?"

"I come from a poker household, J. C."

"Well, I didn't know what it was. She says it's like a mini-tournament. You buy in for a certain amount, everyone gets the same number of chips, and then you play for whatever's in the pot, less the casino's rake. Last Friday the pot at the high stakes table was over $70,000, and it's dollars to donuts that your dad's table is the high stakes table!"

"J. C.," Little Bobby said, his mouth twisted into a frown, "if the pot was $70,000, then the buy-in was probably $10,000. How can we afford the buy-in?"

"Bobby! You exasperate me!" J. C. said, throwing up his arms and walking into the kitchen. He opened the refrigerator door, leaned in, and Little Bobby walked up behind him and pushed it closed.

"Slow down, J. C.," Little Bobby said. "Just hold on."

J. C. took his hands off the refrigerator and put them on his hips. "Bobby, we can't slow down." He put one hand on Little Bobby's shoulder. "Somewhere in that mess they picked up today they've got a set of those plans. You know that. We safely have a few days to pull something off. After that, I don't want to be in the same city with that table. What's the matter?"

"Well, first," Little Bobby began, trying to look at J. C., "it's a crime. It's a crime against the state and, maybe more importantly, it's a crime against the casino. I don't guess you've heard about all those holes out in the desert?"

"Bobby! That's the stuff movies are made of. You don't really think a casino's going to get physical with a cheater?"

"I know what my dad told me," J. C. said, "and I've seen card sharks with bent and missing fingers. But what about jail? This state's pretty tough on cheaters."

J. C. gave Little Bobby that look Little Bobby had seen all his life. He might as well have been daring Little Bobby to go off the ramp on his skateboard, or taunting him when he wouldn't try the slide at the waterpark. "Besides," Little Bobby changed the subject, "where do we get the $10,000 for the buy-in?"

J. C. said, "That's where you come in."

"Where I come in?" Little Bobby said, stomping out of the kitchen, J. C. on his heels. "I'm already in, man. In my house. My schematic. My dad's table. Now it's going to be my money. You're the one who needs to find a role in all this."

"Bobby Bobby Bobby," J. C. said, in his best eighteenth floor voice. "All I mean is that I can't raise all the cash. The bitch has left me lifeless. We've got an opportunity here, a surefire opportunity, Bobby, and it may hinge on you getting a twenty four hour loan."

"A loan," Little Bobby laughed. "I couldn't get a shoe shine on credit."

"Okay, I understand we might have to stretch our imaginations here, Bobby," that statement made Little Bobby grimace with images of mug shots and prison cells, "but let's toss out a few ideas and see what you think."

Suddenly the whole Greensox scenario seemed an easy do.

"First, now promise me you won't over react to any of these ideas. They're just ideas. We're just brainstorming here. First, you could get a loan on the house."

Little Bobby shook his head. "Mortgage my dad's house? I'm not going to do it, and, even if I did, that would take weeks. You got appraisals, surveys, loan approval."

"Okay. You're probably right. But, that's if you went through a legit lender." J. C. raised his eyebrows and cocked his head.

"What? What are you saying?"

"I'm saying there might be some other source, if the vig's right."

"My god!"

"There are people downtown," J. C. said, "and even out here on the Strip who'd make a loan on the deed to this house in a heartbeat."

"And the interest would be 500%!"

"Not if we pay it right back," J. C. said. "It's a sure thing, Bobby."

"They'd own us," Little Bobby said. "Look. We need $10,000 right now, right?"

"At least that."

"I have an idea," Little Bobby said, disappearing into the back of the house and returning, holding up a key, eyes closed, like he was sacrificing an item on an alter.

"What's that?" J. C. asked.

"Safety deposit box. My dad's jewelry is in there."

"Jewelry?" J. C. said. "Watch? Stuff like that?"

"His bracelet, J. C."

"His bracelet? His . . . OH! His *bracelet!*"

Little Bobby nodded, lips pursed. "His championship bracelet. At one point in time," Little Bobby said, "I'd have never parted with it. After seeing that schematic, I'm not sure I care anymore."

"We'll pawn it," J. C. said, "and then we can redeem it."

"Whatever," Little Bobby shrugged.

The two left on their multiple errands about the time the evening buffets opened and returned about the time the stage shows were letting out, J. C. still hyped, Little Bobby tired and uneasy, piling their space age electronic paraphenalia on the same dining room table where they had first examined the schematic.

"Now," J. C. said, "let's test the equipment, and then, you're going to teach me how to play poker."

"You've never played?" Little Bobby asked.

"I've played. I just want you to teach me the way your dad played."

"You're asking the wrong guy, J. C. I'll teach you what I know."

"One thing, Bobby, and I don't mean to be rude or offensive, but, it's about your dad, Bobby. I'm curious. I know he must have won enough money to buy Las Vegas. What happened to it?"

"He *lost* Vegas. Back then jackpots and tournament pots weren't what they are now, but I'm sure he still won a lot of money. He had a few wives who knew how to spend it, too. And he may not have won as much as you think. Are you ready for your first real lesson in tournament poker, J. C.?"

"Sure."

Little Bobby took a deep breath. "Every time you start talking about a 'sure thing' a snake crawls up my spine. First lesson in no limit Texas Hold'Em poker: it doesn't matter what you're holding, and it doesn't matter what the other player starts with, he can still beat you. And, usually, the better your cards, the worse the beat. The bigger the loss. You should have heard some of my dad's stories, J. C.," Little Bobby shaking his head, smiling. "Some of his worst beats came with two Aces in his hand—and the other player starting out with nothing and flopping a flush. My dad had skill, J. C., and now we may know he had more than that, but *luck* is still what wins the pot. I don't care if you know exactly what the other guy's got. He could have nothing and still beat you. If your cards aren't falling, or if his cards are falling, you're not going to win."

"If that's true, why do the same players show up at the same last table every time?"

"You've been watching too much T.V. There are a hundred tournaments a year in Vegas, and the same players don't always win. A small group does dominate. They have experience, a lot of skill, more than their share of luck, and one other thing," Little Bobby said.

"What?"

"They bluff. They calculate the mathematical odds of their own hands getting better, their opponents' getting worse, they read all the tells, and then they just flat out bluff. They bluff on their reputation for very good luck. Novice players play their own cards, experienced players base their play on what they believe the others have, pros convince you that they have something different."

"And you can't tell if they're bluffing until you have all your chips out there."

"Or," Little Bobby said, "if you can see their hole cards on a T.V. screen. I've thought a lot about it, and the way I see it, J. C., my dad's table doesn't guarantee we'll win, or even help us know what to bet. We still can't control the cards that fall. My dad's table just eliminates the bluff."

Little Bobby walked into the kitchen and returned with two beers and a deck of cards. "Now," he said, "let me try to teach you enough so you won't make a complete ass of yourself."

# Chapter Twenty Six

Spike and Oxxie were parked down a sharp embankment from the several outbuildings that constituted the central campus of The Rooster Farm. They called it a campus because the girls could refer to it that way when they wrote home, especially some of the younger ones who were still receiving tuition checks from their parents. The radio was tuned to gangsta rap.

"You know, I came to one of these places one time," Spike said, adjusting the sound in the darkened rental from speaker to speaker and from front to rear.

"I bet you weren't there long," Oxxie said.

"I never really could see the point in it. I mean, if you want sex, you shouldn't have to come to some place like this and pay a lot for it. I mean, what's wrong with just picking up a whore downtown?"

Oxxie nodded, maybe for the first time realizing how stupid he was to have stopped the Doberman.

Spike reached for the paper bag and Oxxie grabbed his wrist.

"Spike," he said, "if you try to do this, pink lace and panties will be falling on the city like confetti. I'm going over that embankment, Spike, I'm going to find Cheeso's car, and I'm going to stick a chunk of plastic explosive on his engine block."

"Don't call him Cheeso," Spike said.

"We're going to kill him, Spike. No need to be polite."

"Pays to be cautious," Spike said, flipping the sound from right to left, bobbing his head to the tune.

"And the reason I'm telling you all this, Spike, over this damn music, is because you should not leave this spot," Oxxie said.

"Oxxie! You offend me!" Spike turned off the radio. "What did the bard say, 'that's the unkindest cut of all?'"

"Yeah, the bard. Well I haven't forgotten how you cut and run at that green light," Oxxie said. "I'm at the corner, jabbing at the walk button, you're hauling ass right through the intersection."

"I stopped," Spike said.

"You got stopped."

"Same difference."

Oxxie opened the door, covering the overhead light with one of his giant mits. He put his thumb and forefinger of his other hand very close together. "Don't move even *this* far."

"Wooooo," Spike said, touching his tongue to his upper lip, "I'm scared!"

Oxxie got out of the car and climbed the embankment in two steps. There were a few weak lights on the windowless buildings aimed at the parking lot, but what was not completely dark was in seriously dark shadow. Oxxie had a penlight on his keychain, but didn't want to use it until he got underneath the big black SUV that Mikey drove. As he approached the car, on tip toes, looking like a giant oak that had escaped its roots and was headed for a populated part of town, the door of one of the buildings flew upon with a metal bang and shrill laughter and a light shower of fluorescent light filled the night. Oxxie ducked behind the SUV. He'd gotten a glimpse of the couple exiting the door, an oval shaped man with a very large bosomed lady who was finding something extraordinarily funny.

As they drew closer, Oxxie got bits of their conversation. "Fuckin' . . . dark . . . fuckin' . . . Berta Mae . . . fuckin'," and believed the man might be Mikey.

Oxxie was still near the rear of the SUV, not the engine block, but reached under as far as he could and squeezed the malleable explosive between a steel chassis bar and the gastank. Then, in a crouch, he ran through the thick shadows and threw himself over the embankment into a multi-stalked yucca plant, while flicking a yellow ribbon off a purple truck.

The woman pointed across the dark lot and said, "My god! Was that a horse?"

"Looked more like fuckin' Big Foot down on all fours," the man said, who let the woman lead him to his car before he invited her into the front seat for one more taste of his pleasures.

Oxxie extracted himself from the yucca plant and limped back to the rental.

Spike was gone. The car was there, but Spike was gone.

"Spike?" Oxxie said in as loud a whisper as he dared, although certain that Mikey was probably too involved with his lady friend to be listening to the night.

"Over here!" Spike said, from the direction of the ground on the driver's side.

Oxxie went around the car to find Spike digging in the sand. "What are you doing, Spike?" Oxxie asked, immediately regretting the question.

"I've lost the damn keys. You took them with you, didn't you? We talked about me staying put and you took the keys with you."

"No, Spike. I don't have the keys."

"Damn damn damn damn damn. Where could I have lost them?"

"How could you have lost them, Spike? You were sitting in the car with them."

After an hour of fruitless search with the penlight, Spike and Oxxie abandoned the rental and began the long walk back into town.

"So, you stuck the stuff on?"

"If you're referring to the explosive, Spike, I did. Not exactly where I wanted to stick it," Oxxie said.

"What does that mean? It'll still blow him up won't it?"

"I think it will, but probably not tonight. It might have to warm up over some hot pavement first. I say we get another rental and visit his place in the morning; follow him until it happens."

"Not too close," Spike said.

Oxxie said, while kicking a desert scorpion off the toe of his shoe, "Right, Spike. Not too close."

When Spike and Oxxie got to Mikey's place the next morning the car was missing.

"Maybe he blew up last night," Spike said.

They drove around the neighborhood and didn't see Mikey, so they drove out to The Rooster Farm, but neither the SUV nor a burned out lump of SUV were in the parking lot. They did notice that a small commune of hippies had moved into their previous rental and were painting sunflowers on it.

When they got back on the highway, out near the giant discount stores and new car dealers, Spike pointed at a big black SUV with dealer's tags, stopped at the traffic signal Spike had just turned red.

"Look! It's Mikey!" Spike said, "and he's driving a newer model!"

They were just in time to see the plume of black smoke rise from the SUV dealership down the road.

# Chapter Twenty Seven

Same old same old for Phillip Riley. A little bit ahead, a few good wins, betting a few more chips after every win, his system du jour, and then suddenly there's a $2000 bet on the table. He had a $2000 bet and he got two Eights. Dealer had a Ten showing. *Same old same old,* Phil thought.

But he said, "No guts, no glory," having already mortgaged both, and then he pushed out another $2000 to split the Eights. A Three landed on each Eight: two elevens.

"Can't stop now," he told a gambler's lie as he doubled his bets on both hands. The hand was worth eight thousand dollars, sixteen thousand total with the return of his original eight, but actually more than that.

Everything he owned, including the pawn tickets for what he once owned, sat in the form of four stacks of black chips on a Vegas blackjack table. What had brought him to this particular point down this strange road, Phil couldn't help but wonder. A high school athlete with three letters, working every day after school at the marina gas dock, four years of college and then another three years of law school. A wife who'd left him and a child she'd tried to take away. That's it! There's a woman to blame? Then, a twist, special training at Quantico for a law enforcement career. His dad's career of choice; a career like a drug that had wrecked his parents' marriage and eventually destroyed his dad.

Phil crawled up out of his chair and stood uneasily at the table. Whatever happened, he told himself, it was *over*. The craziness was over. His career hung by a thread, and his career was all he had, just like his dad, but it was time to salvage whatever he could. He'd go back home and hang out a shingle and work on the gas dock until he got a few clients.

The dealer dealt him two cards on the elevens, both face up and cross-wise. Both were Nines. He had twenties on both hands. A flicker of hope, like mica in the dirt.

The dealer said, "Good luck, sir," and he could tell she meant it. She turned over her hole card, and it was a Six. Dealer had a sixteen: worst possible hand for the dealer. Phil let out the air he'd been holding.

Another player quipped, "You better hope she doesn't have a Five in there!" Phil smiled a sickly smile, wishing the guy would shut up. Hammers pounded his skull.

The dealer dealt her next card. It took a long beat for the number of dots to register in Phil's brain. He was standing with his mouth half open and his eyes half shut, staring at the Seven of Spades, and his mind couldn't seem to do the math until the dealer finally said, "23. Too many," and paid Phil sixteen thousand dollars in white $500 chips.

Phil scooped up the chips and whirled toward his room, almost colliding with Audra Sue, who had stopped to watch the last hand.

"I picked up my chips and I'm headed for my room," Phil said, as if instructing himself, with a pride made breathless by his quick and decisive act.

Audra Sue held her tray under her arm and slowly clapped her hands together a few times. She smiled, lips closed. "And what use do you have for the chips?" Audra Sue asked.

Phil held up the white chips in both hands like Bluebeard, kneading his gold. "What are you talking about? This is sixteen thousand dollars!"

"In chips," Audra Sue said. "Chips are made to *gamble* with, Phil. Why don't you just go over to the cashier and exchange those chips for *cash*. Cash is real money; the type they use in real life."

"Look," Phil said, his pride deflating like a disabled balloon, "I took my chips and walked away!" He elbowed past Audra Sue. "Women," he said.

Audra Sue shook off her disgust, and went about her rounds at the tables.

On the way to the elevator, Phil had a thought. He had a little more than he needed to enter the morning Sit & Go, and he'd heard about some of the high stakes jackpots. With that kind of win he could even pay back those vouchers! He resolved to call the special agent in charge first thing the next morning and reschedule his visit for the afternoon. That morning game could change everything; make everything better.

In fact . . .

Phil turned and retraced his steps to the tables. "Audra Sue," he found her headed toward the bar, "why don't you show up in the morning and watch me play poker. I'm about ready to teach some non-believers what I'm made of." Phil gave Audra Sue his best "I'm Not For Sale" look, turned, and walked off.

"You know," Audra Sue said to his receding image, "My mama was right. Sometimes folks can't get better until they hit rock bottom."

# Chapter Twenty Eight

Little Bobby slipped through a side door of the casino wearing a full beard, wide sunglasses, with a baseball cap pulled low over his eyes, and a black fanny pack with glow-in-the-dark palm trees. He looked like a suicide bomber from an angry foreign faction, or maybe a Reno gambler, but he wasn't fersed, because he didn't look like Little Bobby.

He found a bathroom near the poker tables and settled into the first stall, removing the T.V. from the fanny pack and arranging the headset with an earphone over one ear and a small microphone near his mouth. The earphone was useless: J. C. had no way to talk back, just an almost invisible little earpiece that molded deep into his auditory canal. The actual transmitter fit in a shirt pocket, about the size of one of those transistor radios when only AM stations were popular. The rig had set them back a thousand bucks.

Little Bobby stuffed the beard and sunglasses into the fanny pack with the extra batteries and clicked the T.V. on, extending the antenna. He turned the tuning dial until a clear picture of the table appeared on the screen. As he ran through the next several channels, other views of the same table appeared, allaying the doubts created by their interrupted use of the bar T.V. that only one poker hand would be clearly visible. The fine tuning made the difference.

Checking to be certain the red light on the transmitter was glowing, Little Bobby said, "Mic check. First stall. Bathroom by the staircase." He sounded to himself like a spaceage nerd.

He held his breath for about two minutes until there was one sharp rap on the metal stall door. They had radio contact within the casino.

"How many channels you getting?" J. C. whispered through the door.

"It looks like we have eight or nine on the same table," speaking through the mic. "We still need to verify that we're looking at the high stakes table. Can you get up there?"

"The tables are still roped off, but I have an idea. Watch the screen," J. C. said.

"Which channel?" Little Bobby said, but J. C. was gone.

Watching the T.V. screen carefully, Little Bobby finally saw a coin hit the table and bounce off. "We're on it, J. C. Get registered."

Little Bobby turned off the T.V. to save the battery while the Sit & Go organized, trying to make himself comfortable as he leaned on the hard metal pipes behind him. If he shifted too far sideways, the automatic toilet would flush. He finally removed the beard from the fanny pack and used it as a cushion.

At exactly 9:00, the table host gave the go-ahead and the dealer shuffled and dealt the first round of cards. The game was Texas Hold 'Em. And the rules were simple. Two cards were dealt to each of the seven players on the table, face down. Each could then bet, then three more cards were dealt, called the "flop." More betting occurred, and a fourth card was dealt, the "turn." Then, another round of betting, and the final card was the "river." After the last card was dealt, there was a final round of betting, and the player with the best hand, consisting of the best combination of five cards from their hole cards and the table, won the pot. Each player started with ten thousand in chips, and they played until one player had all seventy thousand. After the house "rake," that meant a pot of about $65,000.00 to the last player standing.

Little Bobby expected trouble keeping up with the hole cards of every player without multiple T.V.'s, but it was amazing, especially after some practice, how well he could follow the whole table. As if to assist, many of the players would look at their cards a second or third time when making a critical call or raise, giving Little Bobby another chance to peek, and another chance to tell. The plan was for J. C. to start slow, dumping all but the best of hands, until Little Bobby got enough practice following the hands and until the number of players diminished to the point that the number of channels were more limited. But Little Bobby and J. C. were rolling at the first all-in show down.

The player to J. C.'s left was a hot shot with a spiked haircut and enough of daddy's money to convince him he was a pro. J. C. drew a Jack and a Ten of Spades, a good opening hand, especially sitting in the small blind. J. C. and Little Bobby had discussed whether Little Bobby should just tell him the players' cards or give specific advise, and they agreed on a combination of the two, but Little Bobby only had a long angle side view of the common cards, putting most of the strategy decisions on J. C. The haircut bet a thousand when J. C. matched the big blind, and everyone else folded except J. C. Little Bobby said, "Two Tens." That was the haircut's cards, so J. C. matched the thousand, hoping he'd hit a Jack and knowing that the haircut might have trouble with a third Ten because J. C. already had one in his hand. The flop was a Jack, another Jack and a Ten. J. C. had a virtually unbeatable full house, Jacks over Tens, and the haircut had a full house, Tens over Jacks. Little Bobby said "All in." J. C. did go all in, and the haircut followed him. The turn and river cards did nothing, and J. C. won the pot and doubled up to what was then about $24,000, and the table was reduced to six players. At the next break, J. C. entered the stall next to Little Bobby.

"I thought I'd be making the decisions," J. C. said.

"That's right," Little Bobby said, "I was just cheerleading."

"How do you think it's going?"

"As well as expected," Little Bobby said. "Now shut up before someone walks in here. Somebody hears us talking they'll check these stalls for a glory hole."

In the next round after the break, two showdowns occurred that J. C. played no part in, and the number of players was reduced to four with a virtually equal number of chips held by each. There was a guy who called himself Nevada Dodson, an old skinny guy with a face like a horse and piercing blue eyes like Albert Einstein. He was a cautious player, and an obviously experienced one. Prying chips out of his stack would be difficult. Then, there was a woman, a hard looking blond with skin the texture of rawhide who seemed to be more interested in positioning her cigarette than playing cards. Her name was Lurlene, and she kept trying to talk to Dodson in a nicotine croak but he'd only nod back. The last player was a loose cannon named Phil who seemed nervous. He also seemed the biggest threat, not because of any visibly apparent edge in skill, but because he was betting big and playing loose and drawing other players into pots that he'd often win on the river with a stroke of pure luck, feeding his appetite.

The next hand caused some heartache. J. C. was in the $2000 big blind, Dodson checked, Lurlene bet $2000, Phil folded at the small blind, J. C. checked, and Dodson folded. That left J. C. and Lurlene. Little Bobby whispered, "Pair of Queens," in J. C.'s ear, a toilet flushed in the background. J. C. had nothing, a Three and a Six, unsuited. And the flop helped no one, an Eight, a Five, and a Ten. Lurlene, apparently attempting to slow-play her Queens, bet another $1000. Little Bobby whispered, "Match it." J. C. sat up straight and glanced in the direction of the bathroom.

"I don't guess I could, uh, take a quick break?" J. C. asked the dealer.

"Ask the table host," the dealer said, and motioned for a guy in a tight black suit to step over. The table host leaned over the table, his hands clasped together behind his back like one of those decorative drinking birds. "Problem, sir?" he said.

"I asked if I could take a short break. I sort of have an emergency," J. C. said, a hand massaging his stomach.

"As a rule, sir, no player may leave the table in the middle of a tournament hand."

"Listen, I'm about to embarrass myself here. I had one of those breakfast burritos and . . ."

Lurlene interceded. "It's okay with me," she said, lighting another cigarette. "I'd rather take a break than see his breakfast."

The host nodded to J. C. who jumped up and trotted off to the bathroom. "What do you mean, 'match it?'" he whispered to Little Bobby when he got into the contiguous stall. "You just made me make a fool of myself."

"She's been folding the biggest hands on the table. She threw in two Aces a couple of hands ago and a pair of Sevens took the pot. Push her, and she'll fold. Everyone who's ever played poker has had a rotten experience with Queens. Stick some chips out there and you'll convince her it's a losing hand."

J. C. shook his head, "I hope you're right. Why couldn't you have told me that when you saw me hesitate? Why did I have to come talk to you?"

"I guess I thought you'd just take my advice."

"I may or may not," J. C. said.

J. C. sat down at the table again, with a weak smile. "Much better," he said, then he pushed $3000 into the pot.

Lurlene did not hesitate to match it. J. C. really did start to taste his breakfast.

The turn card was a Six, giving him a pair: a pair of Sixes against Lurlene's pair of Queens!

Lurlene bet $1000.

The person in J. C.'s ear said, "Bury her!" J. C. reluctantly counted $10,000 out of his stack. Without hesitation, Lurlene went all in. J. C.'s stomach gurgled.

Nevada Dodson leaned back in his chair and laughed. "I've seen some damn interesting tells in my life, but I can't say I've ever *heard* one before!"

J. C. didn't have much of a choice. He could fold, but he already had so much in the hand that it would cripple him, or he could call Lurlene, hoping for a miracle. If he lost, he reasoned, *when he lost*, Little Bobby would just have to come through with another entry fee. "I'm all in," J. C. said, hoping that Little Bobby could see his extended middle finger on the little T.V., their first attempt at casino cheating about to end in defeat.

Both players turned over their hole cards. Lurlene did a doubletake when she saw J. C.'s hand, she smiled, crinkling her rawhide cheeks, already counting the win in her head, but the river card was a Six. J. C. won with three Sixes. "6 6 6," Little Bobby shouted, "I love that hand! Devil's come to Vegas to stick it up a couple of Queens! Woo-hoo!" J. C. heard foot-stomping on a tile floor.

J. C. produced a handkerchief to tap his brow as he stacked Lurlene's chips into his own growing pile. He'd celebrate later, if he could get out alive.

"Did you see that?" the bartender asked Audra Sue, who was standing by his side at the bar T.V.

"How could they have known to go all in?" she said. "Is the dealer in on it?"

"Naw," the bartender said. "I think they just got very lucky."

When Lurlene left, cigarette dangling from a moving mouth, muttering about J. C. and all the dumb luck amateurs who kept her from playing her best game, only three remained. Little Bobby was still shouting, "Who needs a woman when you got a good hand?" J. C. wished he'd shut up.

It was Dodson's turn to be big blind, and Phil called. J. C., grip still a little trembly from the last hand, jacked his $1000 little blind up to $2000.

"This is what I like," Nevada Dodson said. "Everybody in for the flop."

But J. C. lost track of and eventually folded the hand when he heard a sharp rap in the earpiece and a stranger's voice. "You want to step out of there, sir?"

With an abrupt click, all sounds stopped, and J. C. immediately looked in the direction of the bathroom where two men in suits that bulged at the biceps had Little Bobby between them, his feet a few inches off the floor, flying him toward the nearest exit. A ten year old kid stood at the bathroom door, pointing and chattering in the direction of Little Bobby, his parents and another security guard nearby, stooping, mother's eyes wide, dad's fists clenched, the guard shaking his head in disgust, listening to what the kid must have heard in the bathroom.

The bartender pointed toward Little Bobby's ejection across the casino. "Look at that! I have a feeling that contraption around his head isn't a cell phone. Ad guy must have some kind of earpiece and he's talking to him on that thing."

"They're throwing him out?" Audra Sue said.

"I guess that's better than the alternative," the bartender said. "Cheaters aren't usually escorted straight out. They usually have to spend a little time in the basement."

By the time J. C. refocused on the table, Nevada Dodson was sliding his chair back and reaching to shake hands with Phil. "Next time, young man," he promised.

It was down to two, J. C. and Phil, chip totals about equal, and only one could win. Without Little Bobby's help, J. C. could predict who that might be.

The cards were dealt. J. C. drew two Aces! He bet a conservative $5000. Phil matched him. The flop was the Five of Clubs, the Ten of Clubs, and the Ace of Clubs.

At first sight of his three Aces, J. C.'s heartbeat ratcheted up. He went so far as to put his hands behind his chips, ready to push, ready to say "all in," but something Little Bobby had said the night before held up a stop sign. Something about, even with Aces, especially with Aces, you could walk right into a bad beat. J. C. looked at the cards on the table, and realized for the first time that his opponent probably had a flush. *A typical novice mistake*, J. C. scolded himself, getting so wrapped up in his own cards that the obvious was not always seen. All Phil needed were two Clubs, or less if the turn or the river were a Club. J. C. checked.

"Did you see that?" the bartender said to Audra Sue. "Looks like the ad guy is afraid the jerk has a flush."

Phil bet another $5000.

J. C. matched that. The Six of Clubs fell on the turn. J. C. combed his fingers through his hair. Then said, "check."

Phil bet another $5000.

J. C.'s stomach gurgled. He smiled a sickly smile and matched the $5000. The last card to fall, the river, was a meaningless Deuce of Diamonds.

J. C. checked.

Phil leaned back in his chair and said, "all in."

The bartender dashed behind the bar and filled two glasses with tap water. "You saw what the hole cards were, didn't you?" he asked Audra Sue.

Audra Sue nodded.

"Why don't you run out there and take some drinks to our friends?" he said, and winked.

Audra Sue took the two glasses and hurried over to the poker table, where J. C. was still pondering whether to fold a very good and expensive hand. "You gentlemen order these drinks?" she said, and both players looked up. A spark of recognition from Phil; J. C.'s preoccupation was etched into the lines on his forehead. She stuck her finger in her ear and twisted it, then winked. That got J. C.'s attention. Could she see his earpiece?

Audra Sue said to Phil, "You ordered the *Club* Soda. No no. You don't have the Club, your's is the double *Crown*, is that right?" Audra Sue set the glasses down and did an Olympic powerwalk back to the bar.

J. C. looked for a moment like he'd just seen a ghost, maybe heard the ghost of Little Bobby, then his features relaxed into a smile. "All in," he said. "I'll call. I'm all in."

The hole cards were flipped and J. C.'s three Aces beat Phil's two Kings. *Two Kings.* Even with only two players left, Phil's hand was questionable with an Ace showing on the flop, unless he was expecting a miracle on the river! *Loose cannon.*

J. C. jumped up and let out a whoop, sounding a lot like the political candidate he had once advised. He stuck out his hand to shake Phil's but Phil was still staring at the table, lifeless, so he took it back. Then J. C. followed the table host off to the cashier's cage for his winnings.

Phil got up and made a slow wide circle around the poker area in a lost, scrapping shuffle, his chin near his chest, a blush growing up his neck and onto his cheeks. He'd bet his life on that hand. He stopped at the table, picked up and chugged down the "Crown." When he tasted the water he turned his head in the direction of the path that Audra Sue had taken.

# Chapter Twenty Nine

Little Bobby was sitting on the front porch when J. C. got there. He stood up, threw his arms in the air, eyes half shut, and began to holler, "This dumb ass kid walks in, should have been better supervised in a damn casino, starts going from urinal to urinal watching them flush, then I guess he overhears me."

"Something about sticking it up a Queen?"

"Yeah, maybe something like that. And then these two casino Nazi's . . ."

"Bobby Bobby Bobby," J. C. said, pulling a huge roll of green from his pants and waving it in Bobby's face close enough to smell the ink and nicotine. "It doesn't matter, man. We won!"

Little Bobby's mouth dropped open like a fish, wide eyes fixed on the cash. He grabbed J. C.'s arm and dragged him onto the porch and then pushed the door with his free hand. "Inside," Little Bobby said, "I want to hear everything that happened!"

On their second beer, J. C. finally got to the part about Audra Sue. He said, "That was cool, Bobby. I don't know how you talked her into that or even how you contacted her there in the casino. But it worked!"

"What, J. C.? I don't know what you're talking about."

"Sure you do. The Club Soda thing. 'Oh, you have the *double Crown!*'"

"J. C., I really don't know what you're talking about," Little Bobby said.

J. C. explained the incident in detail. "And you didn't set that up?"

"Good news and bad news. Somebody pulled our bacon out of the fire, J. C., but that same somebody knows exactly what we're up to," Little Bobby said.

J. C. pointed at Little Bobby and said, "The bartender! Damn! It has to be the bartender. He must have seen what we were doing with the T.V. that day."

Little Bobby nodded. "I wonder why, though."

"What?" J. C. asked, his adrenalin from the poker win converting into a wave of panic that someone else knew how he'd won.

"I mean I wonder why he helped us. Do you think he wants a cut?"

J. C. nodded. "Oh, I'd say that's a sure bet."

"What kind of cut?" Little Bobby asked.

"Only one way to find out. We'll ask him. I'll go back up there this afternoon and play some video poker in his little tiki kingdom."

"Maybe we'd better wait until he gets off work—meet him outside the casino," Little Bobby said. "Jesus. The guy knows we cheated. Do you think he'll turn us in," Little Bobby's eyes fluttered.

"Well, he is in on it. That thing with the waitress was so obvious that the other player could file a complaint. I'm sure they have it on tape!"

The phone rang in the other room and Little Bobby got up to answer it. When he came back, he said, "You're meeting him in an hour in the hotel pool."

"That was the bartender? He has your home phone number?"

Little Bobby nodded and shrugged at the same time. "And you're not meeting him *at* the pool, you're meeting him *in* the pool."

"What did he say about the money?" J. C. asked.

"He said to put it in a plastic bag."

"All of it?"

"He just said to put the money in a plastic bag and meet him in the pool in an hour." Little Bobby stared off at nothing.

# Chapter Thirty

Spike and Oxxie waited in Mikey's exercise room, watching the T.V. mounted above the stationary bike. A helicopter floated above a local car dealership, taking wobbly aerial shots of what looked like a large charcoal briquet.

> *Authorities are baffled at what is being called a mysterious explosion at a local car dealership this morning. Witnesses on the scene tell us that an SUV in the parking area suddenly caught fire and exploded, sending a column of black smoke over 200 feet into the air. No one was reported injured.*

Spike glanced at Oxxie. Oxxie said, "Slow news day."

Mikey walked in, climbed onto the stationary bike and began to peddle, his flattened nose pointed in the neighborhood of the T.V.

> *There is speculation that this explosion may be linked to the recent attacks by radical environmental groups on the SUV industry, but, at this time, there's no word as to the cause of the explosion. Sources do tell us that lab crews are on the scene and Eyewitness Now will bring you further reports as they develop.*
>
> *Next, a special report: Is there a common food you'll be having for dinner tonight that could cause hemorrhaging and instant death? Details tonight at 10:00.*

Mikey picked up the remote and clicked to a show about dogs joining the Peace Corp.

"Youse guys fuckin' em-bare-ass me," Mikey said, pumping at the peddles of the bike, shoulder hair already matting under the loose tank top. "Three, four days ago, I sent ju fuckin' cocksuckers out ta do a job. A job I might say uv a very pers'nal nat-chure if ya fuckin' know wha' I mean."

Spike turned to Oxxie and silently mouthed, "Nat-chure?" Oxxie whispered, "Personal *nature*." Spike nodded.

"Mikey," Oxxie said, "it shows the respect your brother in law has for you that he's making himself so scarce."

"That fuckin' maggot he betta fuckin' ree-spect Mikey Mozzarelli, or I'll fuckin' learn im some Mikey Mozzarelli ree-spect."

"We've tried to get you that arm, Mikey, but we can't seem to break through the guy's line of security," Spike said.

"Well, see now dat's what I doan unnerstan.' My brudder n law he doan have no fuckin' line uv security. He drives a fuckin' limousine. By hisself." Mikey stopped peddling and checked his watch. Two minutes. He got off the bicycle, motioning for Spike to hand him a bottled water. He took the towel from the handle bars and draped it over his bald fleshy head, sparkling with sweat.

"Two days," Mikey said. "You cocksucker's got two fuckin' days den I call in da fuckin' pro, an maybe he give me da three fer one special. Comprehenso?"

"Comprehenso," Spike said.

Oxxie said. "You want us to spot you on those weights, Mikey?"

"Man," Spike said, "I'm beginning to hate coming here." They were parked in front of Scary Larry's.

"Well, you could wait a few days, and Mikey could take care of that."

"Do you really think he'd kill us?"

"Spike, we lost his hundred and eighty grand. What's amazing is that he hasn't already killed us. We even kill his brother in law he'd probably kill us."

"It's . . . it's . . . ," Spike searched for the word.

Oxxie wondered if Mikey could tell the difference between Spike's and his brother in law's arm.

"It's an affiance," Spike said.

"Spike, I'm not as good at this word power thing as you are, but that doesn't sound right."

Spike said, "It's an affiance made in hell."

"Better."

Oxxie got out of the car and approached the short fence. The front door slammed open and Scary Larry stepped out.

"Where's Honeypie?" Oxxie asked.

"At the ga'damn groomer," Scary Larry said.

"You take her there?"

"She goes by herself. Was that my ga'damn nitro on the news?" Scary asked.

"Yeah. Bad guy traded up."

"Good for business," Scary said, crinkling a corner of his mouth in what may have been a smile. "They show one ga'damn SUV blown up, there'll be three or four copycats before the ga'damn weekend's over. I can make you a better deal on the next ga'damn batch."

"That's good," Oxxie said, "but what we really need is a gun with the next batch. I think there's a good chance the bad guy may want to kill us back."

"Unrefined ga'damn response. What kind of ga'damn gun?" Scary Larry pulled out his little notebook and licked the lead of the stub pencil. "I assume you want a ga'damn handgun?"

Oxxie nodded. "Big, knock down gun."

Scary Larry made a few marks in the notebook. "You expecting more than one ga'damn assailant?"

"I doubt it. Spike and me are pretty simple targets."

Scary Larry nodded. More notes. "No ga'damn metal detectors—that sort of unconstitutional ga'damn shit in the way?"

"Don't expect so," Oxxie said.

Scary Larry turned and walked into the house. Oxxie glanced over his shoulder toward the rental. He thought he heard screaming. Scary returned with two paper bags, one much longer that the other, and handed them to Oxxie who responded with a wad of cash.

"Do you ga'damn floss?" Scary Larry asked.

"When I get the chance," Oxxie said.

Scary Larry raised his eyebrows and nodded a warning, going back inside.

When Oxxie got back to the car, Honeypie was standing on the hood, feet planted wide apart, head aligned with her body in a deadly pointing stance, teeth bared and dripping with foam, eyes yellow, snarling like a wolf eating prey. She pointed at a fuzzy figure in the driver's seat. Dog slobber and muddy paw prints covered every inch of glass, but Oxxie could just make out a wide-eyed Spike, hands gripping the steering wheel, face frozen in a silent sardonic scream, tears streaming down his face.

Oxxie said, "Honeypie!," and the dog flashed him an embarrassed grin and jumped down off the hood, tongue drooping, tail wagging.

After a long good-bye with Honeypie, Oxxie tapped on the wet glass for Spike to unlock the door, who finally pried his fingers off the steering wheel long enough to comply. His face still looked like it was in a windtunnel.

"That damn dog," Spike finally swallowed enough air to talk, "it was like that damn dog in the movie—he tried to eat me right through the car."

"She tried to eat you. That's her favorite movie."

Spike turned on the car and aimed the air conditioner vent at his crotch.

"Look at it this way," Oxxie said, "at least you didn't lose the keys."

# Chapter Thirty One

Harrison Finch plopped the folders down hard on the table in front of Berta Mae Pole as he summarized the content of each one.

"Tommy Harris. Age 58. Chronic liver problems, awaiting a transplant. He meets you in an internet chat room for organ donors. You tell him how brave he is and that leads to how much you'd like to look after him and that begins to cross the line into sexual innuendos. We took it right off the hard drive, Berta Mae. Before long, you're scheduling a meeting and the weekend turns into a week and then it blossoms into a visit to the wedding chapel. You spend your honeymoon wine tasting your way across Napa Valley until he goes into shock from the toxins in his system and has to be careflighted back here to Vegas where he's dead within a week."

"He left a Will," Berta Mae said. "Left everything to his ex-wife."

"Good for him. Then, there's Eli Brown, you mentioned him at your apartment that day. Age 63. Met him on a single's site, and he was from right here in Las Vegas. You must have seen something you liked because he'd had two bypasses. Had a heart that sounded like a go-cart race. You guys hitched up and then you talked him into that apartment above the antique shop. He winds up buying the whole building, and you wind up owning the whole building when his heart blows apart climbing the steps one day."

"He could have lived several more years," Berta Mae said, touching a dry cheek with a tissue.

"In which case you probably would have left him and found another sucker. Like Leslie Chism. Age 49. He had a problem you must have had to research before you found him on the internet. Ollier's Disease. Bones were as brittle as a dried branch. I don't even want to think about how you talked him into riding the big roller coaster on the tower. Came out looking like a bag of uncooked pasta. You got a lawsuit pending on that one. Then, there was Ralph Magers. Age 58. He also had a quality you admired. He was stupid. Stupid and rich: a match made in heaven, right, Berta Mae? You talked him into meeting you for a lover's tryst on the top floor of a Strip casino on the night they were bringing it down with a hundred tons of dynamite. You never showed, and, when they found Ralph, he was still clutching a single yellow rose. Cold, Berta Mae, very very cold."

"Ralphie wasn't so rich," Berta Mae said.

"The one I really can't figure, though, is Alex Sharp."

Berta Mae squirmed in her seat. It was not her nature to stay quiet.

"You met him on the internet, just like the others. You lied to me about meeting him in the Four Winds. You lured him to the Four Winds and then got him to marry you. His poor taste killed him."

Berta Mae made an "s" sound.

"He was morbidly obese; that's what the doctors would call him. But, other than that, he had no life threatening diseases or conditions. High cholesterol, maybe, but he was probably healthier than you. He was just very heavy, and you targeted him for that. See, Berta Mae, that's the pattern in all this. You targeted Harris for his liver, Brown for his heart, Chism for his bone disease, Ralph for, well, maybe Ralphie was just for sport."

Berta Mae smiled and then concealed it with her hand.

"But you targeted Alex for his weight. You knew that bungee cord wouldn't hold him. I'm not sure at this point whether that was just a guess or somehow you really knew, but we'll find that out. And when we find that out we won't be talking anymore."

Berta Mae was quiet.

"You understand what I'm saying? Some people would call you a black widow, Berta Mae. Me, I think that gives what you've done too much personality, mystique. Makes you sound clever. I think you're a psychopath. I think you're a cold blooded common murderer. And I'm going to prove that, and I'm going to get you indicted, and if there's a jury in this state with enough balls to stick a needle in you, I'm going to find one."

Berta Mae looked up, as if from her knitting, and said, "Is that all, Detective Finch?"

Detective Finch shook his head and ran both hands over his hairless scalp. "Just make certain you understand me, Berta Mae. Now, we can talk. Later," Finch pointed at her with his trigger finger, "don't you dare shed one tear on my carpet or I'll add destruction of public property to your charges."

"I'll be careful not to," Berta Mae said, and got up and walked out of the interrogation room.

As soon as she was gone, Harrison Finch went to the men's room to wash his hands. Then to his desk to call Shauna Tell.

"Did you get anything?" she asked.

"I hope not," Finch said.

"You know what I mean!"

"She wouldn't talk. I read her the riot act and she's hard as a rock. I figure she'll probably get lawyered up now. What about Fitzlow? Did you have him over for a discussion?"

"Oh yeah. You know he wears a cape?" Shauna asked.

"Did he tell you anything?"

"I start off, nice and polite, you know me . . ."

"Yeah."

"The minute I ask him whether he knew Berta Mae Pole before the bungee accident, he clams up. Looks at me like I just spanked him on the butt. So I ask him why he's not being cooperative because if I find out something improper's going on I'm going to call up the Bar Association Grievance Committee. At the mention of the Grievance Committee he gets a nosebleed."

"A nosebleed?"

"I say Grievance Committee, his nose starts pouring like a stuck hog. We finally had to call the paramedics. I thought he was going to bleed to death right there in my office."

"So you didn't get to finish your interview?" Finch asked.

"My interview? My god, Harry, I may have killed the man!"

# Chapter Thirty Two

Philip Riley held another one of Special Agent in Charge Herb Cox's yellow number two pencils between his fists. He'd placed the other broken halves back into the pencil cup on Cox's desk.

"Somehow, someway," Phil said, "they knew what cards I had. And not only that, they knew what the other guy *thought* I had."

Cox was a smallish, wiry man, with a grey handlebar mustache, thick white hair, and an easy smile. He'd be more at home squinting over a Montana herd at sunset than riding a federal law enforcement desk, yet it hadn't bucked him off for thirty years. He nodded sympathetically. "Agent Riley," he said, "from what I hear you may need some help."

"I do need help," Riley said. "I think we ought to go in there with . . ."

"No, Agent Riley. I mean *you* may need help. With gambling issues. You don't have to be ashamed . . ."

Riley broke another pencil. "At the risk of my career, Agent Cox, I admit that I got a little carried away over the last several weeks."

"Son," Cox said, "carried away? Like a tsunami carries away a coastline. You lost $65,000 of the Bureau's money and it looks like every cent of your own. This office left over a dozen messages for you and none were returned. The task force gave up on you. I don't really think your *risk* right now is your career. You need to be more concerned if you'll be indicted."

"You're going to indict me?" Riley asked, picking up another pencil.

"*I'm* not going to indict anybody. Unless you break all my pencils. I'm trying to look out for you."

"How can you say I need help? You don't even know me," Riley said.

"I've been in Vegas a long time," Cox said. "Let me make it simple for you. You are as of now on unpaid leave from the F.B.I." He pushed a letter toward Riley, bearing the Director's signature. "You show me proof that you're getting counseling for a gambling problem, and I'll do what I can to get you reinstated. I'll go to bat for you."

"And what about the Four Winds?" Riley asked.

"What about them?" Agent Cox wrinkled his brow. This was not an easy heifer.

"They stole my money, Agent Cox. The Bureau's money! They cheated me out of $65,000!" Riley waved the pencil in the air. Cox made one swift move and grabbed it.

"Look, Phil, I don't know what happened and I think it's pretty far afield right now. I guess you can take your complaint to the police, but let me give you one very sound piece of advice." Agent Cox pointed with the pencil. "Stay out of that casino. You're not on F.B.I. business if you're in there, and I don't see how it can help your gambling problem."

"I'm forbidden to go in there?" Riley asked.

Cox shook his head like he'd tasted something sour and dropped the pencil hard into its holder. "I'm not forbidding you to do anything, Riley. We're talking 'word to the wise.' I said I'd help you if you'd get counseling. If I get a report that you've been in *any* casino during your suspension, I'm going to recommend termination. Right now I guess we can say your problem was brought on or aggravated by your employment, no different than, say, carpal tunnel syndrome for a machine operator. Alcoholism can be job related; why not gambling? But if you keep going to those casinos you're not dealing with the problem, and the whole sorry mess begins to look less like a slip-up by a young agent and more like serious insubordination."

"So they just walk away Scot free? The perfect crime, right? The waitress gives away my hole cards and they bust me out of $65,000 in the most obvious card-talk in casino history and now there's not a damn thing I can do about it?"

"Obvious? How did she *know* your hole cards?" Cox asked.

"I don't know, but she knew, and you can ask anybody there what she said!"

"And you're telling me if she hadn't known your hole cards you would have won?" Cox asked.

"I don't know. I might not have won. You just don't get it, do you?" Riley reached for another pencil but Cox scooted the holder away. "I was cheated!"

Cox said, "I'll make a personal call to the casino. I'll tell security what you say happened. Beyond that, this agency is not involved. One thing I want you to realize—you didn't lose $65,000 in one hand. You lost it over several weeks. *You* lost it. Nobody cheated you out of it."

When Riley opened his mouth to complain, Cox said, "This meeting's over. Put your badge on my desk."

# Chapter Thirty Three

"Over here," the bartender called, waving a single arm in the vastness of the Four Winds pool. He was near the center and neck high in water, his arms sweeping the surface in front of him to keep him balanced.

J. C. kicked off his flip flops and waded down the conch shaped steps and all the way out to where the bartender half stood, half floated.

"You bring it?" the bartender asked.

"The money?" J. C. said, "it's in my swimsuit," positioning his own arms out on the water like a high wire artist to stay upright. The bartender stuck his head underwater.

"Doesn't seem to make a big enough bulge," the bartender said, surfacing, J. C. hoping that sound didn't travel too far over the water.

"That's part of what we need to discuss," J. C. said. A girl screamed and did a cannon ball off the side, a younger boy in hot pursuit. "Why do we have to do this in the pool? Are you afraid I'd be armed?"

"Saw this once in a spy movie. If we had a private meeting away from the casino, you could bring anything. Gun. Wire. Casino could watch us, too. This is the only place at the casino with weak eyes and no ears."

"Except the bathrooms," J. C. said.

"Don't trust your instincts on that one. I heard they pulled a pervert out of one of the stalls today. Looked a lot like that guy you went home with the other night. Besides, isn't the water great?"

J. C.'s arms were already growing tired keeping up a steady tread. "Let's get this over with. You saw the T.V. in the bar the other day, am I right?" J. C. said.

"I did. You are. And you better be glad I did because I was watching your stern this morning."

"I had three Aces!" J. C. said.

"That you almost folded before your drinks arrived."

A bug-eyed, freckled face kid with goggles and snorkle popped up next to J. C. and then submerged. J. C. shook his head. *A spy movie!* "What do you want?" J. C. asked.

"First," the bartender said, eyes on J. C.'s, unblinking, "I want what I won today."

"What? What did you win today?"

"I'd say about $65,000," still unblinking.

"Are you crazy?" J. C. asked. The bartender shrugged. "You want me to hand over the whole $65,000?" J. C. asked.

"For a start," the bartender said.

"I'm not going to do that," J. C. said. "Besides, I've got a partner in this. What do I tell him about his share?"

"You tell him, 'Hooray, we didn't get caught!'"

J. C. looked around the pool, its transplanted palms and lighted waterfall, not appreciating its serenity. "Okay. Look," he finally said, "what if I give you a third? Split it three ways. That's more than you deserve."

"Now, don't get snippy," the bartender said, wagging a water-wrinkled finger. "Whoever *deserves* anything is not the point here. The point is whether I'm going to let my casino, the folks who put bread on my table every week, suffer cheaters to live amongst us. You know what a Las Vegas casino does to cheaters?" the bartender said.

"That's a fable," J. C. said, half smiling.

"Uh huh. And police brutality is a fable: Rodney King slipped and hurt himself? War crimes don't really happen, right? People in power tend sometimes to overstep. And we could be dealing with some very angry, powerful folks here who hire every bad seed that comes out of the N.F.L. Their gorillas work here just before they retire to professional wrestling."

"A third," J. C. reiterated. "If they bring me down I'm taking you and that bar maid with me."

"That is not a nice thing to say. I, however, always try to maintain my civility while I work on my tan." The bartender turned his face toward the sun, squinting, he said, "I'm going to make my final offer, and then I'm going to pee in your pool water. We'll split it 60/40. The money I mean."

J. C. thought about the numbers. Nodding, "That's a possibility."

"I get sixty. You get forty," the bartender said.

"No!" J. C. said, his voice carrying off toward the lifeguard who looked in their direction.

"It's not negotiable," the bartender said, "but, out of an abundance of goodness, I'm prepared to sweeten the pot. I'm prepared to help you turn your, let's see, the $26,000 you'd have left, into a cool million."

"What are you talking about?" J. C. asked.

"You ever play with one of those fortune telling balls? You turn it over and it reads, 'the answer is not yet clear.' Something like that. Well," the bartender put his hand to his forehead, Swami like, "the answer is not yet clear. But it will become *crystal* clear when I get the sixty percent, the $39,000."

J. C. felt like the sun was baking his brain. "All I have with me is half," he said, "$32,500. We'll agree on 50/50," he said. "You take what I have right here and tell me your little secret. And, *I'll* sweeten the pot. In one week, I'm gone, and the whole gig is yours. And I'll even tell you the names of the other casinos with bogus tables," something J. C. wished *he* knew. A stone cold bluff.

"Other casinos?" the bartender warbled. "You drive a hard bargain ad man, just don't make me reach into your swimsuit for the cash. The lifeguard may get jealous."

J. C. handed the bartender the plastic bag who stuffed it into his loose shorts. "Now," J. C. said, "tell me about your damn crystal ball."

"Veejay's coming," the bartender said, simply.

"Veejay?"

"Veejay is the whale among whales. Veejay plays one game: poker. And Veejay never leaves the high stakes table. On a weekend, he'll win or lose two million, maybe more."

"When?" J. C. asked.

"His private jet gets here day after tomorrow. He usually goes straight to bed and then pops up at sunrise to play poker. It should be easy to get on the table at that hour."

"That's nearly three days. We may not have that long," J. C. said.

"Why?" the bartender asked.

"Let's just say our chances of discovery increase every hour." J. C. wasn't ready to reveal the CrestLine records predicament.

"Well, *c'est la vie*," the bartender said, pushing off for a swim back to shore. "I'd cut it pretty close for a couple of mil."

J. C. stood alone in the middle of pool, treading water, legs cramping, his neck turning pink in the sun, half as rich as when he'd gotten in. "Such is life," he agreed.

# Chapter Thirty Four

"Hey Audra Sue," F.B.I. Agent-on-Leave Phillip Riley said, "what's up?"

"Why are you calling me?" Audra Sue asked, one hand on the phone and the other balled into a fist on her hip.

"I just want to talk," Phil said.

"About what?" rotating to see if anyone was listening.

"Look, Audra Sue, I've been a real ass. I admit that."

Silence, so Audra Sue said, "But now you're better."

"I just want to see you," Phil said.

"You were an ass this morning, but now you're better? I don't think so, Phil."

"Don't hang up! Can't we just meet and talk?" Phil asked.

"Talk about what, Phil?"

"Talk," Phil said. Audra Sue could hear shifting on Phil's end of the phone, creaking like he was sitting up off a bed. "I hit bottom today, Audra Sue. I'm wiped out. I've lost my job. There's only one person I know in Las Vegas, Audra Sue, and that's you."

"Is that it? You want a *loan*?" Audra Sue asked, like tossing a dart.

"No, I don't want a loan. I just want to talk. I'm afraid, Audra Sue. I'm afraid I might do something crazy."

"What are you talking about, Phil?" Audra Sue slowed her tapping foot and listened.

"I just don't have anything left. I've," Phil stopped, blew his nose, "I've lost everything I've ever worked for."

"Maybe you need to go see a doctor, Phil. You need to talk to someone who can help you," Audra Sue said. "I don't know how to help you."

"Will you call someone for me, Audra Sue?" Phil asked.

"Just call anyone. Go to the emergency room. I don't know."

"Will you go with me, Audra Sue?"

"Phil, I work. I can't just take off work and go with you to the hospital. You just need to go there and tell them you need help."

"Will you go with me after work, Audra Sue?"

"I don't know," Audra Sue said.

"Audra Sue," Phil said, voice a little too serene, eerie, "remember when you and Bill used to come down to the marina with Cyndi and me and we'd all walk over to Beggar's Hill together and take a bottle of that terrible strawberry stuff?"

"I remember, Phil," Audra Sue said, carefully.

"Those were good times, weren't they Audra Sue?"

"They were good times, Phil."

Sobbing. "I'm scared, Audra Sue. I'm scared I want to do something or take something. I've never felt like this. I just want to rest, Audra Sue. I just want to lie down and close my eyes and rest. I don't want any more of this mess I've caused."

Audra Sue blew out a "whew" between tight lips and said, "Alright. Meet me outside the casino in two hours, Phil. I'll take you to the hospital."

"Oh, Audra Sue. You'll never be sorry. I promise you that," Phil said.

"I already am," Audra Sue said, after she hung up.

# Chapter Thirty Five

"You gave him *half* our money?" Little Bobby asked.

"I didn't just give it to him. It's not as simple as that. He wanted all of it," J. C. said.

"He wanted all of it so you gave him half," Little Bobby said.

"He was going to the casino, Bobby. He'd rat on us and they'd never touch him. Those goons would break our legs, Bobby."

"Ahhh. You laughed at me when I mentioned holes in the desert, J. C. What changed your mind?"

"All we need is one more good game, Bobby, and the bartender told me about a guy: a million dollar poker player by the name of Veejay—have you heard of him?"

"My dad may have talked about him."

"We just need a way to get you in there with the equipment," J. C. said.

"Jesus, J. C."

J. C. waved off concern. "We've got some time to figure it out," J. C. said, turning his face away as if about to be punched.

"What do you mean, *time?*" Little Bobby asked.

"This Veejay guy doesn't get here for two days. We'd play the next morning," J. C. said quietly, with a little shrug.

"J. C.! That's three days! We can't wait that long! Marcuso may have those other schematics right now!"

J. C. held up his palms. "Bobby, if he had them, we'd know about it. Do you think if he pulled something like that out of your dad's stuff you wouldn't be the first to know? He'd have someone over here knocking on your door right now!"

There was a loud knock at the door. The floorboards creaked when Little Bobby's and J. C.'s feet relanded. Both bent into a crouch, arms out for balance. Lungs still.

Another knock. Little Bobby slipped out of his loafers and tiptoed into the front hall, easing down the wall until he could peer out a tall rectangular window next to the door. He carefully pulled the sheer drape aside and looked out, into the piercing black eyes of Detective Harrison Finch. Little Bobby showed all his teeth in a big smile and then let go of the drape. "Jesus," he said, before he let out a breath and opened the door.

"Can I help you, sir?" Little Bobby said, measuring his words, like a drunk at a D.W.I. stop.

Harrison Finch pulled out his badge and a pain tightened around Little Bobby's chest. "I'm Detective Harrison Finch, Las Vegas Police. Are you Bobby Crest?"

Little Bobby said, eyes mostly closed, eyeballs fluttering, "Junior. I'm Bobby Crest, Junior. Robert Crest was my dad and he was Robert Crest, Senior. I'm Junior. I'm Little and he was Big. I don't know very much about my dad's business." A terrible thought suddenly crossed Little Bobby's mind. "You're not here about that kid in the bathroom are you?"

Finch was reeling. "Should I be?"

*Oh crap*, Little Bobby thought. "Uh. No. Of course not. That was some kind of misunderstanding. Ha Ha." *Oh crap.*

"Well," Detective Finch said, "we'll get to that." There was a sound of a back door closing. Finch craned his neck into the hall. "Anybody here with you?"

"No, I don't think so. Not anymore," Little Bobby said.

"Anybody else live with you?" Finch asked.

"Nope," Little Bobby said.

"Do you mind if I come in?" Finch asked.

Little Bobby stepped aside and Finch walked in, eyes scanning every inch of the hall as he entered. Little Bobby pointed toward the couch in the living room. "You want to sit down?"

"Sure," Finch said. Finch studied the room like there'd be a test and then took a seat in the middle of the couch. Little Bobby stood in front of him, balancing on the balls of his stocking feet, glancing toward the interior of the house. "You want to sit, too, Mr. Crest?" Finch said, making the same kind of sitting motion with his hand that he used with his dog.

"Thank you," Little Bobby said, and sat on the edge of a chair.

"Now tell me about that bathroom problem," Finch said.

"That *is* why you're here. God. I'm, uh, sitting in a stall in the bathroom at the casino . . ."

"Which one?" Finch asked.

"The very first one," Little Bobby answered.

"No. Where was this bathroom?" Finch asked.

"At the Four Winds." Little Bobby stopped and frowned. "This isn't why you're here, is it? If it was you'd know where it happened."

Finch said, "Guilty! But tell me about it anyway, Mr. Crest."

"I'm just sitting there cursing and yelling about some poker game and a kid walks in and it scares him. He runs out and tells his parents and security carts me out of there. That's the honest tuth. That's exactly what happened." Doing the eye thing again.

"Is anything wrong with your eyes?" Finch asked.

"No."

"Ok. Well. I'll check back at the station but I don't think there was a report made by the parents. I don't remember one, anyway. I'll just keep our discussion in mind. I want to talk to you about something else, Mr. Crest."

Little Bobby nodded, trying to force his edgy eyes to stay open.

"I understand that your dad owned CrestLine," Finch said, "and that Victor Marcuso has, for whatever reason," *because the kid's a duck*, Finch assessed, "taken the CrestLine records into his possession through a court order."

"That's right," Little Bobby said, "and maybe that's good because I really don't know what's in those tables, I mean, records. I don't know what's in those records," Little Bobby said.

"Right. The reason I'm here, Mr. Crest, is sort of a long shot. Have you ever heard of a woman named Berta Mae Pole? Or, just Berta Mae. She keeps changing her last name."

"Oh, my god!" Little Bobby said, smiling. "I haven't heard about that big bosomed witch for years. Who's she married to now?"

"You know her," Finch said.

"She threw me out of my own house! If my dad hadn't had a Will when he died she'd be living here right now instead of me."

"Your dad was married to her?"

"About a year before he died," Little Bobby said.

"How did he die?" Finch asked.

"Heart attack," Little Bobby answered. "His doctors used to say he was a heart attack waiting to happen."

Finch nodded. "And Berta Mae was married to him when he passed?"

"You know, I really don't think so. I got a call from my dad to come back and move in and that was right before he died. He thought she was back to whoring; that's all I really heard him say about her. His ex's were never a topic for discussion."

"Whoring?" Finch asked.

"I'm sure my dad's rolling in his grave, but he met Berta Mae at the Rooster Farm. That place out in the sticks?"

"I know the place," Finch said, recalling a particularly bloody homicide that the county people had sought his help on, "and he met her there."

"He met her there and paid for her boob job."

"Really?" Finch said. "To hear her talk, they're real."

Little Bobby laughed for the first time in a long time. "To hear her talk, she's real."

"Do you know if your dad ever discussed the business with her, Mr. Crest? Let me simplify that. You know about the bungee death at the Four Winds."

"Yes," Little Bobby said.

"We believe that Berta Mae was connected with that."

"Connected?" Little Bobby asked.

"She was married that same day to the victim and she, let us say, encouraged him, enticed him, to jump. Do you know if your dad ever discussed that bungee cord or anything associated with it around Berta Mae?"

"No. I was shut out after the marriage. I don't know what they talked about. I'll tell you this, though," Little Bobby's voice quivered a little, "my dad was a big talker. They didn't call him Big Bobby for nothing. He probably talked about every shrewd deal he'd ever made and every client he'd hoodwinked."

"So, you think your dad sold defective goods?" Finch asked.

"Not really, but he was a businessman, you know? He liked to knock back a few beers and talk about his conquests and the other guy's stupidity. Especially the other guy's stupidity. Like it was really funny. This guy ordered sixty watt bulbs that won't be bright enough in the upstairs halls, that guy ordered recycled linens, and they'll unravel in a month. You know—that sort of thing."

"This guy ordered a bungee cord, and it's defective?" Finch suggested.

"Never heard that," Little Bobby said.

"And he'd talk about these things to you often?" Finch asked.

Little Bobby glanced at his socks. "No, he never really talked to me that often."

"Yeah, well, I appreciate your information. It's very helpful. And if you think of anything else give me a call." Finch handed him a card. "I think Berta Mae knew there was something wrong with that bungee cord and she may have gotten that from your dad."

"Would that mean the Four Winds would sue me?" Little Bobby asked.

"I'm not part of that, but I don't see anyone succeeding in a lawsuit if Berta Mae set this whole thing up," Finch said.

"Will you tell Victor Marcuso I'm being helpful?" Little Bobby asked, almost panting.

"I'm tell him," Finch said, rising. "Now, do you mind if I use your bathroom before I go?"

Little Bobby shook his head and said. "Down that other hall. To your left."

Detective Finch counted the toothbrushes when he got there, and the damp towels. He flushed the toilet and left.

# Chapter Thirty Six

At another casino just up the Strip a tightly clad young French lady flew a great distance through the air and grasped a metal bar firmly with both hands. But, her hands finally tired, slipping down and off, and the only question was not whether she would fall, but whether there might be a net to catch her.

Down the Strip, at the Four Winds, Audra Sue waited just past the cab stand on the wide entry drive, hanging there for Phil Riley. In contrast to her cocktail outfit, she wore jeans and a simple tee, looking soft and lost as she checked her watch and scanned the moving groups for a sight of Phil. He came up from behind her, looking as crushed and misshapen as the last piece of bread in the loaf.

"Hello, Audra Sue," he said.

She turned quickly, "There you are! You're late. I didn't know whether to call 911 or just go on home."

"Sorry. I took time to make some calls."

"Listen, Phil, you don't need to talk to me. You need to see a doctor," Audra Sue said, a little too loud. Tourists in clip-on shades glanced their way.

Phil nodded. "I called a rehab place called Brookhill," Phil said, "its all the way out of state."

"That's good," Audra Sue said. "I think you should get away from here," taking a slow breath, letting it out, Phil watching. "So. I guess you don't need me to take you to the hospital."

"No, I guess not. I'm going up to Brookhill tonight. Can I call you from there?" Phil asked.

"No, Phil. I really wish you wouldn't call me," Audra Sue said.

"Can we just, like, go into the coffee shop and talk for five minutes?" Phil asked.

"No," Audra Sue said.

"I'll make a deal with you. You give me five minutes and I'll never bother you again. I won't call you or write you from Brookhill. I'll leave you completely alone."

Audra Sue clenched her fists.

"I can be pretty persistent, Audra Sue. Five minutes, and it's all over."

Audra Sue hesitated, loosened her grip, and said, "Ok, but not in the casino." She gestured toward a low slab of pigeon spotted concrete where they could sit. "Five minutes, Phil." She led the way to the slab, her stomach ached.

"So why are you so afraid of talking?" Phil said, following and sitting beside her, his thigh touching hers. His thigh touching the $16,250 folded into her pocket.

"Look, Phillip," Audra Sue said, sliding an inch away, "I'm the one who said hi to you the other night in the casino and you just ignored me, pretended you didn't even know me, then, I met you in the bar, and you ignored me again, *humiliated* me, Phil." Audra Sue hated that feeling of tears trying to seep through the words. "Then, last night, I suggested you cash out and quit while you were ahead, and you smarted off about how great you are at poker. I don't have any room for you right now, Phil. It's hard enough, you know?"

"I know," Phil said, "I'm really sorry," somehow moving a little closer as he said, "that's all in the past, Audra Sue."

Audra Sue looked at Phil, a question in her eyes. "*Past* is right, Phil. You act like there's some sort of—relationship. We have no relationship, Phil. You understand that, don't you?"

"Well, there is a *connection*, isn't there?"

"Connection?"

"We're friends, aren't we?" Phil asked.

"We know one another."

"And as a friend, Audra Sue, will you tell me something?"

"What?"

"How did you do it? How did you know my cards?" Phil asked.

Audra Sue got up and started toward the main casino entrance. Phil grabbed her right arm above the elbow and held her in place. His fingers made deep colorless indentations on her light skin. "Don't walk off, Audra Sue." Phil's voice was calm and resolute. "I want to know how you knew."

Audra Sue tried to pull her arm away but the fingers tightened. "You're hurting me, Phil! You want me to yell for security?"

"I don't think you'll do that, Audra Sue. I think security would love to hear my story. You know who I work for, Audra Sue? The F.B.I."

"You're crazy. Show me your badge!"

"I don't have to show you anything."

"Phil, you're crazy. You're nuts. *Let me go!*"

Phil released some tension in his grip, but held on. "That's pretty funny telling me I'm crazy, Audra Sue. You're the one who can prove I'm not crazy." Phil stood up next to Audra Sue, pressing himself against her. She could feel his heat and smell the sweat on his shirt; feel his angry breath. "*You're* the one who can tell me I'm *not* crazy, Audra Sue. You knew my cards, didn't you? Tell me I'm not crazy—tell me you knew my cards!"

"Go to hell, Phil." She pulled her arm away as a group of oriental children under the loose supervision of a Korean crone suddenly encircled then and flowed on past. One little girl with hot-fudge eyes looked up at Audra Sue the same way she'd looked at the young French lady on the overhead bar. "You deserved it, Phillip Riley!" Audra Sue said, "I'd do it again." Audra Sue covered the distance between Phil and the nearest taxi before Phil could get another grip, her upper arm already bluing. He watched her as she gestured toward the driver from the backseat and the taxi sped out of the circular drive.

Phil took the microrecorder from his shirt pocket and shut it off.

# Chapter Thirty Seven

Berta Mae and Mikey lay side by side on a round purple waterbed, a thin sheet pulled over Berta Mae's mountains, Mikey in the hairy altogether.

"You sure can fuckin' move, Berta Mae," Mikey said, chest heaving, sucking in air, glancing at his watch—the second hand.

"It's my magic thang, sweety. You always know how to move me, Cheeso."

Mikey gritted his teeth. "Didja get dere?" Mikey asked.

"Always, Mikey. Same time as you," Berta Mae said.

"You fuckin' get dere faster than any lady I ever screwed," Mikey said.

"It's all you, baby. All you."

"Now," Mikey said, "tell me bout dat fuckin' detective."

"Harrison Finch," Berta Mae said.

"Finch: sounds like a fuckin' tweety boid."

"He's trying to lay some murders on me," Berta Mae said.

"Whoja fuckin' pop?"

"No, nothing like that. You know that guy got killed on the bungee jump at the Four Winds?" Berta Mae asked.

Mikey shook his head. "Dat musta been da newspaper dat got stuck in my commode."

"Some guy went off the tower at about 500 pounds. Rubber broke, and it's supposed to be *my* fault."

"Doan make no sense," Mikey said, hand scraping at his crotch. "Why dey pin it on you?"

"I was married to him. They say I made him take the leap."

"See! Right dere!" Mikey said. "Didn't da fuckin' marriage guys knock out dat *obey* part—just stop, right afta love an' honor?"

"I still like that in my vows, Mikey. 'Love, honor, and obey. Until death do you part.' I think that's the way it should be."

"Well, jew'd know betta dan me, Berta Mae. So, dis fuckin' detective, dis Finch guy, he leanin' hard?"

"Oh, yeah. Wants to indict me and try me for first degree murder."

Mikey crawled out of bed and pulled on his trousers; pulled the strapped tee shirt over his head. "I got dese two fuckin' guys deys doin' a job for me now an' maybe dey can pay dis fuckin' tweety boid a visit."

"*Threaten* him are you saying?"

"Maybe jus' make it fuckin' clear Mikey doan wan' his friends hassled, ya know? See, da good part—dese guys is disposable."

"Expendable?"

"Yeah, if it doan work, if dey get plugged or somethin', dat's fine, an I disclaim any fuckin' knowledge."

"Mikey," Berta Mae said, "let's hold up on dat, that plan right now."

"You jes let ol' fuckin' Mikey know, willya Berta Mae?"

"I will, Mikey. I promise." Berta Mae pulled Mikey down across the bed for a kiss while he was trying to button his Hawaiian shirt. "Where're we going on my birthday, Mikey? You haven't forgotten my birthday?"

"Oh, fuck," Mikey said, standing back up, causing storm waves in the water bed, "dat's da day after fuckin' tomorrow?"

"What are we doing, sweetie?"

"Oh. You're meetin' Mikey at da Four Winds. You're watchin' me lay waste to some fuckin' Indian poker player with too much money for his own fuckin' good. Den we may pay a Mikey Mozzarelli visit to da fuckin' jewelry store."

"Oh, Mikey!" Berta Mae squealed. "You're too good to me." She pulled him down again onto her breasts, his head getting a little trampoline action off her left one while saying "Gotto fuckin' go, Berta Mae."

When they stepped into the dark parking lot, Berta Mae said, "Look, Mikey! There's that horse again!"

"Fuckin Big Foot," Mikey said, "runnin' on all fuckin' fours. Lookin' fuckin' familiar."

# Chapter Thirty Eight

Victor Marcuso's Senior Vice President for Casino Operations was named Emory Sirkel, and was about as circular as a human being could get. Short round legs supported his round body, all somehow expertly clothed by a tailor with extraordinary round talents. A round head grew on his round shoulders, deeply tanned and thinly lined with black, stringy hair. Even his eyes, traversed by round, horn-rimmed glasses, were themselves quite round, and his mouth, which often made a little round "O" when he talked, was, of course, round. But, lest round be considered soft, or timid, if Satan were round, he would still be no match for Emory Sirkel. Sirkel's mind worked like one of those legendary tikatock creatures, methodical and completely devoid of emotion. In fact, despite his shape, Sirkel was nicknamed The Sickle during a series of devastating job cuts. They usually just called him The Sirkel.

"So, what have you found?" Marcuso asked, certain Sirkel had found something or he wouldn't be seated in the office. Sirkel held several pieces of aging legal size paper protruding from a letter size folder. A spot of a spider crawled across the drooping edge of one.

"Two things," Sirkel said. "We uncovered an old brochure, an advertising document, showing the specs for the bungee cord. It's actually signed by our purchasing agent and indicates the model we purchased. That matches the number on the actual cord."

"The model?" Marcuso asked.

"Yes," Sirkel said, already a bit impatient, "the model. There were two models to choose from. In terms of tensile strength, that's the resistance of a material not to break under pressure . . ."

"I know what that is," Marcuso said.

"The models are essentially equal. Both the 920 and the 920UA are tested at 1500 pounds. That doesn't mean they would break at 1500 pounds. That means that the material could begin to stretch, distort at that weighted tension."

"But that's simple pulling pressure, right? I mean, it would hold a 1500 dead weight easily, but there would be some additional multiplier of pulling pressure because of the drop off the tower."

"Oh yes," Sirkel said.

"Based on that, would you have stepped off that tower with a 1500 tensile strength cord?" Marcuso asked.

Sirkel smiled a little half moon smile and answered without hesitation, "Never."

Marcuso had a chilling premonition of old Everhard asking that question of Sirkel on the witness stand. "So, we screwed up, didn't we? We should have posted weight limits."

"In retrospect," Sirkel said, "that would have been very wise. But that's not the real issue in this case."

"And what is?" Marcuso asked.

"We've got more serious problems," Sirkel said. Was he smiling? "The purchase order stapled to the brochure and the brochure itself show that we ordered the 920 instead of the 920UA, the 920 cord and harness being several hundred dollars cheaper, and our cancelled check shows the lower, 920 purchase price."

"I thought you said they both had about the same tensile strengths," Marcuso said.

"They do, but there's one big difference. Care to reason it out?" Sirkel said, crinkling one round cheek in a smirk.

Marcuso thought for a moment, pushed back from his desk, silhouetted by the window looking out onto the pool. It was late afternoon, and, as usual, there was just a wisp of a cloud on a cerulean sky. A blazing Las Vegas sun baked the huge patio and its patrons as in a raging stone oven, and ignited the shimmering pool water like a sea of fire on a parched and arid planet.

Before Marcuso could answer, Sirkel said, an impatient professor to a slow student, "UA treated. That's the difference. The 920UA was coated with a substance that protected the rubber from the effects of ultraviolet rays created by the sun. The 920 did not have that protection, and over time, a constant exposure would make it brittle, non-elastic, reducing its tensile strength to very dangerous levels. Very dangerous levels, indeed."

"And, that would amount to negligence on the part of the casino?" Marcuso asked what was surely a rhetorical question.

"*Gross* negligence," Mr. Marcuso. "It wouldn't have taken a 500 pound pull on that cord to break it. That just made the result a certainty. It was a deathtrap waiting to be sprung." That smile again.

Marcuso stood at the window, his back to Sirkel. He watched a young boy in baggy trunks, shrieking with excitement and dripping with water as he ran down the edge of the pool, squeezing his inflated water mattress under an arm. "Who knows about this?"

Sirkel knew that question was coming. He had served Marcuso for too long. "A temporary worker we hired for the project found the brochure and purchase order. His instructions were to just set aside all items dealing with the Four

Winds or bungee jumping. He did that, and I'm certain he didn't take the time
to pay much attention to its contents. They were working fast, simply separating
paper. I'm the only other one who saw it."

"And, other than in this office, of course, you haven't discussed it with
anyone?" Marcuso asked. The kid outside threw the mattress onto the water and
jumped for it, landing just long enough for it to flip over and dump him squealing
into the pool.

"That's correct."

"Then leave it on my desk, Mr. Sirkel," Marcuso said, with his back still
turned.

"I have another matter here I want you to look at. Something I personally
uncovered in the records," Sirkel said, raising the folder.

"Just leave it all on my desk, Mr. Sirkel."

Sirkel hesitated a moment before he rose, but, finally put the folder on
Marcuso's desk and waddled out of the office. Definitely smiling.

# Chapter Thirty Nine

"What did he want?" J. C. asked, stepping carefully through the back door into the kitchen.

"He was a police homicide detective," Little Bobby said.

"Be serious, Bobby. Was he from the casino?"

"No, J. C., he wasn't from the casino. Did you think he was in here breaking my legs?"

"He was a police detective? What did he want?"

"He was asking about one of my dad's ex-wives," Little Bobby said. "That guy who got killed on the bungee jump at the Four Winds? They think she had something to do with it."

"Scared the hell out of me," J. C. said, opening the refrigerator door for a beer.

"Yeah," Little Bobby said, "I could tell," heading toward the living room.

J. C. followed. "We need to talk, Bobby. We need to figure out how we're going to do this Veejay thing."

Little Bobby plopped himself into the middle of the couch and spread his arms over the back cushions. "I'm not sure I want to do anything, J. C."

"What are you talking about? This is our chance to hit one big score before they find out about the table and close us down!"

"One big score. Those words bring up images of tall grey walls and communal showers. You remember how you felt when you heard that knock on the door, J. C.? You ran like a scared rabbit." J. C. took a long pull on the beer. "We're not cut out for this sort of thing," Little Bobby said, shaking his head.

"Bobby, I told you that game this morning was a sure thing, didn't I? And it was. We made over sixty thousand dollars!"

"And gave away half of it," Little Bobby interjected.

"Now we're looking at over a million!" J. C. drained the beer and set it on an end table. "That's life altering, Bobby. That's worth some major risk. Can you imagine what you could do with that kind of money, Bobby? Only thing you'd have to give up would be groveling. No more groveling, ever again."

"You made big money in that Wall Street firm, didn't you? What happened to all that?" Little Bobby asked.

"Houses, boats, it was great, Bobby. Power. But I mortgaged my future by marrying my best client's daughter. She found a way to make a downpayment with everything I earned." J. C. exited to the kitchen and came back with two open beers, handing one to Little Bobby then sitting on the edge of an overstuffed chair, facing him and speaking almost reverently. "This money's different, Bobby. This is free money. No strings. This is new-start money. Do-what-you've-always-wanted-to-do money."

Little Bobby's vision of grey walls began to shift to the sight of a green pennant flying over a baseball stadium. "A million might not last too long in this town," Little Bobby said.

"I agree," J. C. said, "but it's a helluva good start. While people are telling you what money can't buy, don't let them ever tell you that money can't buy respect. It does, and with any brains and a little luck you can grow that little feature into its own money tree, especially in this town. One word, Bobby: *leverage*. That's what you don't have. And, speaking as someone who once had it, Bobby, you definitely want some of that."

Little Bobby let out a resigned sigh. "You must have been really good at what you did." Then he turned up the beer and drained it. "Let's just try not to get caught," he said.

# Chapter Forty

"You sound like that old Greek, searching for an honest man. Turn off the light, Diogenes," Shauna Tell chuckled, holding up an imaginary lantern against the darkness, "and go on home."

"Why does everyone need to lie to me?" Finch said.

"Because you look like you'll hurt them if they tell the truth," Shauna said. "Surely he wasn't lying about Berta Mae."

"No, but he was hiding something, and I swear I heard someone else in the house before I knocked."

"Maybe Bobby and Berta Mae started doing the horizontal tango after daddy died," Shauna suggested.

"He seems a little too healthy to get mixed up with her. But he's up to his ears in something, and he might bear watching," Finch said.

"Well, hopefully not by you. We've all got enough on our plates right now," Shauna said. "There's got to be a full moon. Things are getting crazy. I had a visit from a young guy, *F.B.I. agent*, raising hell about some big poker scam at the Four Winds. He tried to play me a recording of some cocktail waitress he's accusing of knowing his hole cards."

"F.B.I. agent?"

"I called Herb Cox and he said the guy's on non-paid leave. When Montana Herb says some guy needs counseling he must be pretty far gone."

"Sounds like trouble," Finch said.

"Then, I get into this weird situation with Emory Sirkel," Shauna said the name with a sneer.

"Sirkel. Marcuso's operations chief?"

"Right. For years. I call up Sirkel and ask about the CrestLine records," Shauna said.

"The ones they confiscated from Bobby Crest," Finch said.

"Now don't be too hard on your future employer."

Finch rolled his eyes. "Why Sirkel? What's his involvement?"

"His name is all over the court order. 'Take and deliver these such and such records to Emory Sirkel, Four Winds Casino.' Well, I asked Sirkel if we could send a guy from our office out there to assist in the search. Actually, you know me, Harry, I didn't ask his permission. I told Sirkel we were sending a guy. Sirkel says 'What records? What search?' I tell him his name was on the writ that the sheriff delivered and he says there must be some mistake. Says he knows nothing about the CrestLine records."

"Odd. Did you call Victor Marcuso? Maybe Marcuso wants inquiries to go through his office."

"Man, Harry. Someone lies to you and you want to put them under surveillance. With me it's just 'odd.' A misunderstanding."

"Sorry."

"I think it's worth a visit. Somebody needs to go out there and tell Sirkel that we have more right to those records than the Four Winds," Shauna said. "Bust his chops."

"I'll do that today," Finch answered, absently.

"What's up?" Shauna asked.

"I don't know. I was just thinking. Why did they want all those CrestLine records in the first place?" Finch asked.

Shauna raised her index finger to impart the proverb: "If you want it done right, do it yourself. They needed something quick. They didn't trust Bobby Crest to find what they needed in time, or to find it at all."

"Fast answers," Finch nodded. "Lawsuits don't break land speed records, Shauna. A lawsuit could go on for years. A plaintiff would have two years to even file a lawsuit. I don't think that's the reason at all."

Shauna leaned back in her creaking chair, a smile forming on her face. "What are you suggesting, Harry Finch? Espoiliation? A cover up? You think they might try to conceal something?"

Finch shrugged, frowned. "It just seemed like they tried to grab everything before anyone else could see it."

Shauna's eyes sparkled in the flourescent light. "They're looking at a fifty million dollar lawsuit," she said. "Even if Berta Mae craters as a plaintiff, some family member will pop up. Negligence by a big casino means big money, and if someone can prove they knew about a problem and allowed it, wow, they don't want those odds."

"You know, I really don't care what sort of Rambo tactics they use in the damn lawsuit. I just don't want them interfering with a police investigation, a *murder* investigation," Finch said. "They're going to find themselves in the same cell with Berta Mae if I get one hint they're hiding something."

"What cell, Harry? She's not cell-bound yet."

"She will be," Finch prophesized.

Harrison Finch was waiting in Emory Sirkel's outer office within the hour. He loomed over Sirkel's secretary/receptionist, a fish of a woman with too much lipstick and big ears that reminded him of gills. Finch guessed that she was very efficient.

"No, I do not have an appointment. No, this cannot be discussed on the phone. No, I am not going to take a seat and wait until your boss can see me. I need five minutes with Mr. Sirkel in his office and you do not even want to hear the alternative."

The secretary opened her big red lips, but Sirkel stepped through his office door before the confrontation continued.

"Mr. Finch," he said, "your reputation precedes you."

"Good," Finch said, and was led by Sirkel into a large but sparsely furnished office, where Sirkel waved a round little hand toward one of two high-back chairs in front of an oval desk.

"Have a seat, Mr. Finch," Sirkel said, placing himself on the edge of the other chair. "How may I help you?"

"The CrestLine records, Mr. Sirkel. Do you have access to them?"

"You're asking a question, Mr. Finch, that best could be addressed by Mr. Marcuso."

"Okay," Finch said, "get him on the phone."

"What?"

"Get Marcuso on the phone. I want to see the records, and if he needs to authorize that, let's get his authority."

Sirkel glanced at the phone on his desk and seemed for a moment to be about to use it. Then he said, "That probably won't be necessary. I think I know what Mr. Marcuso would say. If you'll follow me, Mr. Finch."

Finch followed Sirkel out of his quarters and down a long corridor of separate offices and finally to a steel metal door that led to a concrete staircase. At the top was another corridor, with more offices and a large conference area covered with plastic sheeting and littered with rusting filing cabinets and scattered folders. Three young guys in shirt sleeves shut up and jumped up when Sirkel entered. "We need the room, gentlemen," Sirkel said, and all three workers slid past the men at the door. They stood in the hall, quiet and wide-eyed, so Sirkel closed the door.

"They didn't seem to be looking very hard," Finch said.

"Well, we've been through every shred of paper and we found nothing of value," Sirkel said.

"Really? Nothing at all?" Finch asked, thinking of Diogenes. The cynic.

Sirkel stuck his arms out, cruxifiction style. "Nothing," he said. "Nothing at all about the bungee cord."

"So why do you need to keep these files?" Finch asked.

"Uh. We don't. We'll be returning them. Forthwith."

Finch took in the room. He or someone from his department could go through the files, but that seemed worthless. Either Sirkel was truthful and nothing was there, which seemed doubtful, or documents had been removed.

"I'll need the names and contact information of everyone who searched the files," Finch said. "I'm going to want to talk to all of them."

"That's fine," Sirkel said, "but why?"

"Let me ask you something, Mr. Sirkel. You ever spend time in jail?"

His mouth formed that little "O."

Finch pointed his finger at Sirkel's chest. "I want to make myself very clear. I don't really care what you do to protect yourself in a lawsuit. If I go looking for corporate ethics I'll look somewhere other than in a casino. But this is a murder investigation. You lie to me or you lie to anyone who's part of this investigation *again,* and there's not enough money on this Strip to keep you out of jail."

Sirkel started to speak, but changed his mind.

The Homicide Division at the Stewart Avenue law enforcement building was almost empty when Finch returned to his office. A young man in shorts and an AC/DC tee shirt sat with his back to him in the metal chair beside his desk.

"Are you lost?" Finch said, as he got to his desk, and then recognized Jimmie Taylor, the kid from the bungee jump. "Sorry, Jimmie, you have a little bit more color than the last time we met."

"Greg called me from the casino. We worked together on the files. He told me you were there with The Sirkel today."

"Okay. What's up?"

"They had me working on the files because the bungee jump was shut down so I didn't have anything else to do. Greg said The Sirkel told you nothing was found. That's not true. We found something."

A shiver swept up Finch's spine and ended in the tiny hair on his neck. "What did you find, Jimmie?"

"I didn't find anything, but one of the other guys found a bunch of stuff. The only reason I'm telling you is because I strapped that Sharp guy in that night and I don't want anyone saying I screwed up."

"No one's saying that."

"This stuff we found, it made me feel better, you know, that I didn't do nothing wrong and all. I've thought a lot about what happened."

"What was found, Jimmie?"

"It was like an ad, with two different cords. One had some kind of stuff painted onto it like they put in suntan oil, you know, like sun protection. The other one was cheaper. And the casino bought the cheaper one."

"You saw this ad with your own eyes, Jimmie? Someone didn't just tell you about it?"

"I saw it man. I touched it. Then The Sirkel comes in and grabs it up and swore us all to secrecy. Had us sign something and said they'd prosecute us if we told anyone. Can I go to jail for telling you this?"

"On the contrary, Jimmie. You may be the only one who doesn't. You're doing the right thing," Finch said.

"The only reason I'm doing it is because I feel so bad for that guy. And because it's the truth."

"You ever hear of Diogenes, Jimmie?"

"Who's he? Is he a cop?"

"I'll tell you about him sometime. Right now I want you to meet a friend of mine who's a lawyer in the District Attorney's Office."

"They won't give me a drug test, will they?"

# Chapter Forty One

"I'm not setting up in some bathroom stall again." Little Bobby and J. C. walked on an elevated walkway between casinos, keeping their conversation at a level of intensity just below public comprehension.

"We ought to try that new steak place at Schaherazod," J. C. said. "Ha! I wonder if their poker tables are fixed. You know what we ought to do? We need to offer our services to the casinos to debug their tables. Charge then a fortune to take a portable T.V. into each one."

"Be better than what we're planning," Little Bobby said.

"You know, I was thinking . . ."

Little Bobby instinctively edged an extra few feet away as they walked.

"Who worked with your dad?" J. C. asked.

"What do you mean?"

"It's not a one person operation, Bobby. Someone had to help your dad read the cards. Inside guy; outside guy. Who worked the outside for your dad?"

"I never thought of that," Little Bobby said, stopping so an electronic door could fully open, bathing him with refrigerated air.

"Did he have a trusted employee working for him, or a close friend who hung around?" J. C. asked.

Little Bobby took a few steps to think and then stopped at a spot-lighted wall display for a live Vegas show, a tall shapely dancer with a carnivale hat. "There was this one guy," Little Bobby said, "Cholo was what my dad called him. He helped with some of the deliveries. Cholo had a big white van." Little Bobby laughed. "He was very protective of that van. I thought he was just afraid I'd break something. Maybe it was decked out like a spy movie inside."

"So where is this Cholo?" J. C. asked.

Little Bobby shook his head. "Haven't seen him since my dad's funeral."

"We could try to contact him," J. C. said, stepping on the moving sidewalk, Little Bobby following.

"I guess his name could be in the business records," Little Bobby said. "I don't even know if he'd be the guy."

"The outside guy?"

"Yeah. He just always went with my dad to the poker tournaments. They'd go in the van," Little Bobby said.

J. C. and Little Bobby stepped through the front entrance of the Four Winds, met immediately by the clanging, ringing, and calliope tunes of a metal sea of slot machines.

"I never thought I'd be walking in here again," Little Bobby said, looking around like he'd never seen the place.

"Where are we supposed to go?" J. C. asked.

"The guy from operations said to call security from the front desk and they'll take me to the files." Little Bobby stopped so suddenly that he almost fell forward. A slot player plowed into him from behind. "You don't think this is some sort of trap?" he said, recovering. "They know about the schematics and they're luring us back here to beat the crap out of us?"

"No, Bobby, I don't. They know where you live, Bobby. If they really wanted to they could come in the middle of the night and beat the crap out of both of us. All you're supposed to do is check the file cabinets, sign that they're all here, and then they'll bring them back. Isn't that what they said?" J. C. lowered his voice: "You know what this means, don't you Bobby? It means they haven't found anything about the table."

"Right. I just hope it's not a trick."

Security met them at the front desk and led them to the file room. Loose papers and files were still strewn around the room and stacked on the file cabinets.

"Wow," J. C. said to one of the security men, neither of whom had carried Little Bobby out of the bathroom the day before, "you never know these . . . uh . . . catacombs exist. All these offices and work areas. It's a little city. Like, where are we right now?"

"We're right above the casino," the security man mumbled an answer.

"Yeah, well, pretty much the north end of the casino, right?" J. C. asked.

"More towards the middle. Look, you just need to confirm that all the files are here, okay," the security man said. "That's our instructions. Mr. Sirkel said it's very important that you verify we haven't kept anything, taken anything out. You need to sign this." He held up a one page document on a clip board.

"Well," J. C. said, "you're asking the impossible. We can't sign that until we put these loose files back in order and then go through it all to see what's here."

The security guy looked at J. C. like he was planning where to bite him. Finally, he jerked his cell phone off of his belt and stepped out of the door. When he stepped back in, he said "You have twenty four hours."

J. C. said, "Thank you, but, we really need forty eight hours."

A deep, gutteral growl. Little Bobby glanced behind him, but it was coming from the throat of the security man.

He jerked his phone off his belt again.

J. C. raised a hand to interrupt. "Forty eight hours *from* tomorrow morning."

RON USELTON

The security man gritted his teeth and stepped out to dial. When he stepped back in, "The Sirk . . . Mr. Sirkel says thirty six hours."

"From tomorrow morning," J. C. asked?

"Yeah. Thirty six hours from tomorrow morning. You come back then, you can get in, but we ain't letting you in and out every couple of hours."

"Well, that's okay, then. We'll come in tomorrow night, Bobby here will, get the files straightened out, don't need any help with that, then he'll be out by noon the next day. Not bother you again."

"Yeah," the security man said, banging the clip board down on top of a file cabinet. "You saw the way we got here. Give them my name," pointing at his name plate, "if anybody asks. Just be sure you sign this thing before you leave, that we haven't removed anything."

Little Bobby nodded. J. C. leaned over and whispered, "We got a home."

# Chapter Forty Two

"I'm leaving," Audra Sue said.

The bartender silenced the blender. "No you're not, girl! You haven't been here long enough to leave. You have to get weird and jaded first."

Audra Sue was in her street clothes. With her big round shades and hair down around her face, she looked like a regular tourist. Or a lady on the run. "I've got a little money, thanks to you; it's not like I've got any roots here. I'm going out to L.A. and just see what develops. Maybe I'll even go up the coast."

"Big bad Vegas scare you off?" the bartender asked.

"It is big and bad. Security called me in today and said someone with the downtown F.B.I. office called them."

The bartender motioned Audra Sue behind the bar where he turned the blender back on. "Scary. What did they say?"

"Nothing much. They said someone from the F.B.I. office called because one of their agents reported he got ripped off at the poker table."

The bartender let out a low whistle. "You think that squirrel was a feebie?"

"Sometimes, I have no idea what you're saying."

"The gambler. Cool Hand Puke. Mr. Double Crown. He was an F.B.I. agent?"

"I don't know. I met him outside the casino and he said . . ."

"Wait! You met him?"

"He tricked me."

"Maybe you *should* depart us. That wasn't the wisest move, sweet pea."

"Like you. Standing in the middle of the pool. That was real smart?" Audra Sue asked with a grin.

"I saw that once in a movie," the bartender said, eyes averting.

"I hope you didn't pay much to get in."

"So, what did he say, the guy you met, like a total idiot, risking your life, outside the casino?"

"He said he was with the F.B.I. So, I asked to see his badge, and he didn't show it to me."

"Probably lost it on the blackjack tables. But then the F.B.I. called our security people?"

"Yeah, so maybe there was something to what he said."

"What did you tell security?"

"I told them the guy was a real nut case. He told me he was checking himself into a mental hospital. And I told them all I did was deliver drinks to the table. Then I went straight up to the personnel office and quit."

"Did you say anything about me?" the bartender asked. The blender was beginning to smoke.

"Just that you're a real nut case."

"No."

"That's right: 'No.' I didn't say anything. I just acted creeped out that somebody would blame little ol' me for knowing their hole cards."

"Weird they'd think that," the bartender said.

"Jaded. Weird and jaded."

"Well, if you're leaving, that means you won't be able to play," the bartender said.

"Play? Play what?"

"I just had this wild, crazy idea that you might want to play a hand of poker." The blender stopped. Forever. The bartender turned on the water. Hard.

"What do you have in mind?" Audra Sue said.

"Saving a whale," the bartender said. "In about a day, Veejay comes to town. He's going to play poker, and our two friends from the bar the other night are going to try to beach him. Sorry for the fish metaphors, but, they fit, you know?"

"Whales are mammals."

"I know that. Anyway we sort of, help the very rich mammal. No kidding? Whales are mammals?"

"So, what's in it for us?" Audra Sue was smiling.

"A reward. Beyond your wildest dreams."

"I have pretty wild dreams," Audra Sue said.

"Remind me to pursue that concept with you at some point. How much would you pay to keep from losing millions?" the bartender asked.

"A lot," Audra Sue said.

"That's what we're going to get. A lot," the bartender said.

Audra Sue folded her arms. "If I do this, just promise me," she said, "you won't make him get into the pool."

# Chapter Forty Three

The next morning a purplish dome covered the valley, supported by stalks of jagged lightening. From Carver's Plateau, a lofted outcropping of slate and desert hardened sandstone, Spike and Oxxie could view the Mozzarelli house and the complete mansion studded wasteland that surrounded it. Rain water turned the fashionably winding dirt roads to mush and the manicured ravines were raging streams. It glistened from the Spanish tiles on Mikey's roof. Light rain is not an option in the desert. A rain cloud is so rare, when it comes, it seems intent on just dumping its payload and rushing off, as if concerned it might be recognized so far off course, an interloper in the wrong neighborhood.

"This gonna lower the temperature," Spike said, wide-eyed at the huge drops slapping the car's hood.

Oxxie wore a fleece jacket with the collar turned up around his neck. "Prob'ly cool off a tad," he agreed.

"And," Spike threw his arms up at the elbows like he was signaling a touchdown, "the bomb won't blow."

"Uh huh, but the desert, it'll get hot again. Bomb's not going anywhere except where the car goes."

"What about the gun, Oxxie?"

"What about it?" Oxxie said. "You're not asking to mess with it again."

"We got a bullet left," Spike said. "We could go down there and finish him off right into his cornflakes."

"Mrs. Cheeso is there."

"She'd probably be glad we did it."

"That's a chance I'm not going to take," Oxxie said.

"We could shoot him, and then hand the gun to her," Spike said.

"I saw one time in a movie," Oxxie said, smiling, "where the bad guy put the gun in the wife's hand and made her pull the trigger. Maybe we could sneak up behind her."

"I think I saw that movie!" Spike said. "Is that the one where they meet in the hotel pool?"

Oxxie raised the binoculars to his eyes. "White van. Pulling up to the house. Two magnetic ribbons. One guy getting out and going to the door."

"You know who that could be?" Spike said. "That could be the damn hit man, cuttin' a three for one deal!"

"Could be," Oxxie said, binoculars still focused. "A triage."

"What does he look like?" Spike said.

"Like a long way off. We better just watch our backs for a white van."

"What kind?"

"That kind with the shoe box chassis, big cam, and short, lift-back hood." Spike looked confused. "Like they transport prisoners in."

"Oh, yeah!" Spike said.

"Only this one might be a little easier to spot," still peering through the binoculars. "Got enough antennas on top to troll for birds."

"Hmmm," Spike said. "Maybe he's a storm spotter."

"Yeah. Probably a pretty high demand out here in the desert for that."

Within the hour, Mikey came out and both men climbed into the back of the van, then, both got out and went back inside the house. Spike and Oxxie waited in the rain until both vehicles left the driveway nearly two hours later.

"Strange," Oxxie said, watching through the binoculars as the van turned toward them and then Mikey's car followed it out of the driveway, "looks like a handicapped parking permit hanging from the mirror."

"What's strange about that?" Spike said.

"Mikey stuck one on his SUV, too."

# Chapter Forty Four

Veejay's flight from New Delhi was met at the charter terminal by four Geishas, his request, a newly tailored suit by a Rodeo Drive tailor and a bottle of Veuve Clicquot-Ponsardin. A thin man, his features unwrinkled but becoming increasingly more angular with time, he wore a loose fitting cotton running suit that almost exactly matched his latte complexion. He carried a bag that looked like a doctor's bag attached to his wrist by a silver chain and combination lock.

From the charter terminal, he traveled directly to the Four Winds. The limousine was black, instead of the white one he'd requested, so he opted to ride with one of the oriental women in her little white compact, so the trip took nearly an hour.

Veejay went straight to his room at the Four Winds, an upper floor suite with a separate bedroom for each of the Geishas. Dinner was delivered at 8:00, and no one but room service would see Veejay until he emerged the next morning.

Meanwhile, Mikey and Cholo sat in the rear of Cholo's van in a handicapped parking area next to the main casino. Cholo had nine T.V.'s tuned to different channels and mounted into a console. Mikey hadn't really believed Berta Mae when she told him about Big Bobby's association with Cholo, so this was the "seeing is believing" session, and seeing what Mikey saw on the T.V.'s was definitely believing. Hearing was believing, too, when Mikey heard Cholo's voice on the tiny earpiece.

The men made arrangements to meet in the same spot at sunrise the next morning, Mikey handed over a thick envelope, and got out of the van and back into his SUV for the drive home. Spike and Oxxie followed him out of the parking lot and all the way back to the residence, getting lost only three times when Spike took shortcuts to avoid traffic signals and the one time he got behind an oriental lady in a white compact and had to drive fifteen miles per hour.

Meanwhile, Little Bobby and J. C. entered the casino through the main entrance at about sundown, Little Bobby carrying an attache case. They were never asked for I.D. or stopped for interrogation while they retraced their earlier route to the file room, although they were certain their presence was registered and tracked through the security monitors. When in the file room, both searched the area for surveillance cameras, and found none, and the outside door for a lock, and it did have one. Little Bobby opened the attache case and brought out the portable T.V., clicked it on, and got a perfect view of an unknown player's hand at the high stakes table. J. C. stuck up his palm for a high-five, and Little Bobby reluctantly returned it. J. C. left, and Little Bobby went about arranging some files into a makeshift bed, checking carefully for spiders.

Meanwhile, Harrison Finch spent lunch and most of the afternoon with Shauna Tell and an investigator from the D.A.'s office, composing and drafting affidavits for search warrants and an arrest warrant. Finch planned to get a judge's signature before the day was out, or, at the latest, first thing the next morning, so that he could storm the offices of the Four Winds for whatever records might still exist and whatever persons might be directly or indirectly responsible for the offense of, among others, Obstruction of Justice. His objective: to shut the casino down by buffet brunch the next day. Shauna Tell warned him to stay away from any judge with a known penchant for casino gaming and/or buffet brunch. That was not an easy task.

Meanwhile, Audra Sue and the bartender stood in the hotel pool, arms sweeping the water like surfacing mermaids, Audra Sue rolling her eyes, discussing an elaborate strategy and code. She claimed to have a good working knowledge of poker from watching celebrities play the game on T.V., so the bartender spent a good deal of time talking about how the basic game was played by real people with a modicum of intelligence and their own money at risk, while trying not to seem acerbic. They had to take a short break for the bartender to bribe the kitchen help to allow him to take the dinner tray up to Veejay.

Meanwhile, Emory Sirkel went to bed early but was awakened by a thought that popped up suddenly through the still water like a old sunken buoy; a thought that had been slowly surfacing ever since he had turned the documents over to Victor Marcuso. It was in the form of a "what if," and it involved those diagrams he had found, those curious schematics of poker tables located at Schaherazod, World of Luck, and The Legacy. What if a table at the Four Winds were similarly rigged and the schematic was simply missing? Marcuso could worry about how he would inform the other casinos about the find, but it was Sirkel's job to check out their own tables. He would do his job, first thing tomorrow.

Meanwhile, F.B.I. Agent-on-Leave Phillip Riley cleaned his firearm.

# Chapter Forty Five

The morning of the next day started before sunrise.

Mikey and Cholo slid into two handicapped parking slots just outside the casino closely tailed by Spike and Oxxie. Mikey's big black SUV was still in one, unscorched piece. Once inside the casino, Mikey and Berta Mae approached the rope at the high stakes table and waited. J. C. Martin was already there. He nodded at Mikey and Berta Mae who were engaged in an animated discussion regarding what she might do to him after the poker game. Audra Sue wandered up, a sickly smile on her face and over $30,000 in her purse. J. C. glanced at Audra Sue, and did a double-take. He opened his mouth to speak and she turned away. All of them waited at the rope.

Casino personnel met Veejay's arrival with a quickening of pace, patronizing smiles and elaborate greetings. Showing a smile that stopped below his eyes, Veejay stepped past the velvet rope as it was unfastened by the table host. Wearing his new suit but unbuttoning his shirt collar and loosening his tie a bit, Veejay sat at the table directly across from the dealer. The table host stepped back to the rope, which still kept the riff raff out.

"Cash game, ladies and gentlemen," the table host began. "Mr. Veejay's rules. Maximum five players. Minimum buy in of ten thousand. The game is no limit Texas Hold'Em. Blinds are $500 and $1000." Then, the velvet rope was officially lowered. Mikey took a seat in the first chair to the left of the dealer, J. C. slipped in between Mikey and Veejay, Audra Sue took the chair to Veejay's left, and a young man sat to Audra Sue's left. He wore a light jacket zipped up to his throat and a baseball cap pulled down to his brow. The fraction of his face that could be seen around his large sunglasses looked puffy and raw.

"Good morning, Audra Sue," Phil Riley said.

Audra Sue sat in a posture of purposeful rigidity; she jumped at the sound of her name. Turning her head quickly her mouth involuntarily dropped open. "Phil?" she managed to say, "What are you doing here?"

"Playing poker, Audra Sue. Just playing poker." Phil put $10,000 in new bills on the table in front of him to purchase chips.

"I thought you said you were broke," Audra Sue said, wanting suddenly to get up and leave.

"The miracle of plastic, Audra Sue. Never leave home without it."

She took the $30,000 from her purse and put it on the table. Phil glared at it as it was converted into chips and the chips were stacked in front of Audra Sue.

Veejay held up one finger and the dealer slid a million dollars in poker chips across the table. Apparently, whatever was in the black bag Veejay carried from the plane was already credited to his account.

J. C. bought in for $30,000, wondering how many times he'd have to double up to get Veejay's stack.

Mikey was a little slow on the draw. He seemed to be talking to himself. Mumbling, "Fuckin' so much noise . . . fuckin' chips . . . how can I fuckin' . . ." almost like a kid absent-mindedly singing along with the music on his boom-box earphones.

Berta Mae stepped over, leaned down, and kissed Mikey on the cheek, whispering something intense into his ear. He clamped his mouth shut with one word, "Fuck," searching the faces of the other players, a silly grin on his face, he put $50,000 on the table for his chips.

"Turrett's," Berta Mae explained to the table as she rose from Mikey's side, and then darted for a side door. Spike and Oxxie, watching from a nearby row of slots, glanced at one another.

The dealer fanned the cards across the table and said, "High card draw for the button."

Everyone reached for a card. Phil caught the Ace of spades and got the dealer button. He smiled at Audra Sue, "Just a taste of what's to come," he whispered.

J. C. said, "Aren't you the guy from the Sit & Go?"

Phil straightened his sunglasses and didn't answer.

With Phil on the button, Mikey was the small blind and J. C. was the big blind. The first round was dealt. Veejay was the first to act and called, matching the big blind. Audra Sue folded, as did Phil. It was Mikey's turn, who had a strained look on his face. He kept looking at Veejay's cards, still face down on the table, and then back at his chips.

"You gonna fuckin' look at dem cards?" he finally said to Veejay.

Veejay smiled, and acted like he'd never heard him.

Mikey spoke to the dealer, pointing toward Veejay. "Ain't he spose to fuckin' pick up and look at his fuckin' cards before he bets?"

The dealer shrugged.

"Fuck," Mikey said, raising the bet on his two Tens by another thousand.

J. C., too, was watching Veejay, but said nothing. Finally he raised $5000 on his two Jacks.

Veejay folded, never once looking at his cards.

It was Mikey's turn, to either match J. C.'s $5000 or fold. He was mumbling to himself. Finally, with a gesture toward the table like a karate chop, he said, "Fuckin' fold!" J. C. took the first pot.

Little Bobby said into J. C.'s earpiece, "Did you see that? It's like Veejay knows what we're doing and he's messing with us. Or warning us."

Veejay was big blind for the next hand. Audra Sue folded, Phil matched the big blind, Mikey called, J. C. folded. Veejay joined Phil and Mikey in the pot by checking, without looking at his cards.

"What if ya got a pair uv fuckin' Aces?" Mikey said.

"What if I do?" Veejay asked, with a movie star smile.

Mikey shook his head so hard his cheeks clattered. "I need a fuckin' bargirl! Let's get some fuckin' drinks over here!"

The flop was King of Spades, Queen of Clubs, Ten of Diamonds.

For the first time in the game, Veejay looked at his hole cards. Both Mikey and J. C. unconsciously stuck an index finger to their earpieces at the same time, as if the move were choreographed. Phil watched the strange ballet over the top of his sunglasses. Mikey muttered something under his breath.

"What did you say?" Phil asked across the table.

Mikey raised his eyes and realized Phil was looking at him. "You fuckin' talkin' ta me?"

"What did you just *say?*" Phil repeated. "Did you say something?"

"Fuckin' nuttin," Mikey said. Berta Mae was back, hoping Cholo was warning Mikey to shut up.

Veejay bet $10,000. Phil hesitated. Phil had a pair of Tens in the hole, making three Tens, but calling Veejay meant that he'd be all in, and with a King and Queen showing, and Veejay betting heavy, Veejay might have the winning set. After another torturous minute, Phil folded.

Mikey folded, "Pair a' fuckin' Kings," he said, under his breath. Berta Mae shook her head.

J. C. called, but, when the turn produced another King, J. C. folded.

The usually very silent Veejay said, "Like the Christian carol. We Three Kings," revealing to any observant player that he'd only had a pair after the flop. The third King had not come until the turn.

Phil shook his head as if to clear it, remembering Mikey's clairvoyant little comment before the third King fell, wondering if it were just a good guess. He felt like he was standing off, everyone else in on the action.

The next hand brought the big blind over to Audra Sue, and she carefully stacked $1000 in chips on the table.

"Play much poker?" J. C. asked her.

"Other people's hands," Phil interjected.

Audra Sue just smiled weakly and nodded.

"You look so *familiar* to me," J. C. said.

Phil laughed out loud. "You can cut the charade if it's for my benefit," Phil said.

J. C. looked at Phil. "What in the hell are you talking about?"

Audra Sue took her index finger and made a little circular motion on the side of her head that Phil could not see. J. C. nodded reluctantly and was quiet.

The cards were dealt and Phil, Mikey, and J. C. all called. Veejay turned his small blind of $500 into $1000 and also called. Audra Sue hesitated until she realized she already had $1000 in the pot because she was the big blind. "I check," she said. She gritted her teeth as she realized she'd almost made a fool of herself by trying to fold with $1000 already bet.

The flop was the Six of Hearts, the Seven of Hearts, and the Ten of Hearts.

Phil checked, Mikey bet $10,000 with the usual growls and grumbles, and J. C. called the $10,000. Veejay folded. Audra Sue was about to fold her marginal Five of Hearts and Jack of Clubs, when the bartender stepped up.

"Did I hear someone ask for bar service?" he said, specifically to Audra Sue, "Can I interest you in a Mimosa, M'lady?"

Audra Sue looked at him, incredulous. He nodded back.

"Gimme a double fuckin' bourbon," Mikey said.

"Coffee," J. C. said, winking at the bartender, who winked back.

Veejay, keeping his eye on the bartender, declined a drink. Audra Sue said, "I guess I'll have that Mimosa." Phil was silent.

When the bartender was gone, Audra Sue won the table's full attention by saying, "I'm all in." She pushed her remaining stack of nearly $30,000 to the wager line.

Phil shook his head and tossed in his cards. "It's hell being short-stacked," he said to Audra Sue. "I could play a lot better with some of those chips."

It was Mikey's turn, and he was apparently in some sort of violent internal argument with himself. "Fuckin' ain't got . . . fuckin' hearts . . ." Then, he looked up with fire in his eyes. "All in," he said. As soon as he said that, he grabbed his ear, as if someone had just shouted into it. Audra Sue's heart pounded as J. C. and Veejay folded.

Little Bobby said into J. C.'s ear from upstairs: "There's not another Heart in the hole. I don't know what the bartender told her but Hearts are due!"

The dealer instructed Mikey and Audra Sue to turn their hole cards face up. Mikey held two Sixes in the hole, Audra Sue her Heart and Club. Another Heart appeared on the turn. It was all Audra Sue's game unless a miracle occurred, and it didn't. She doubled up to over $60,000 with her flush. Risky, but profitable.

Mikey groaned. "I love dem fuckin' sixes," he said, a youngster with an empty cone, his ice cream on the floor, and a little mouse squeaking loudly in his ear, Mikey pulled out more cash. Berta Mae placed her hands on her hips.

# Chapter Forty Six

Victor Marcuso gestured Detective Harrison Finch to a chair but Finch remained standing, backed up by two uniformed officers. He handed Marcuso a thrice-folded set of papers.

"Can we talk in private?" Marcuso asked, nodding toward the officers.

Finch relented, sending his armed assistants to the outer office.

Finch then took the seat he'd been offered. Little Lenin sat at his desk.

"Now tell me what this is all about?" Marcuso said.

"We have a search warrant for the casino," Finch said. "We have information that you found papers on the bungee cord that are relevant to our murder investigation. Your Mr. Sirkel says nothing was found, which, in my opinion and I think a grand jury will probably agree, is a blatant lie and amounts to obstruction of justice."

"A grand jury?" Marcuso asked. "You're going to take this that far?"

Harrison Finch took a deep breath. "We're going to take this to the wall, sir."

Marcuso teepeed his fingers at his chin. "You know," he began, "I've been very impressed with your investigation, Detective Finch. You've been quick and thorough; not let a stone go unturned."

"Thank you."

"We could use you here at the casino, I mean after this whole ugly mess is laid to rest," Marcuso said.

"Yes," Finch said, "I imagine you could *use* me."

Marcuso didn't flinch, searching Finch's face for what he wanted. "Well?" Marcuso said.

"Well, what?" Finch asked.

"Will you consider my offer?" Marcuso asked.

Finch stood up. "Right after your trial, Mr. Marcuso."

"Fi-nn-ch," Marcuso said, lengthening the consonant, his arms conducting an invisible orchestra, "consider who we're dealing with here. Berta Mae Pole, some grifter whose been married more times than all of the Gabors put together. That damn Fitzsomething. That lawyer with gold dust for brains. Is that who told you about the brochure, Finch? That damn lawyer?"

"I never said it was a brochure," Finch said.

Marcuso slapped his desk, rattling the pictures of his ancestors. "You're a piece of work, Finch. How exactly do you intend to execute a search warrant on a casino?"

"Well, if we feel that the integrity of the search is being jeopardized, we'll put up crime scene tape and shut you down."

"You son of a bitch! There's not a judge in this state who'd let you search our gaming floor."

"We won't need to do that if we find what we're looking for up here."

"And what exactly are you looking for, Finch? You probably still can't tie this back to Berta Mae Pole," Marcuso said.

"Berta Mae Pole is secondary right now. I've been lied to in the course of a murder investigation," Finch said. "You don't seem to want to understand that."

"You're crazy. You know that? I know about L.A. You can start searching in here, right now. This is a witch hunt, Finch, and, not *if*, but when, *when* I get your badge, I'm going to hang it right up there on my wall."

"It'll look good there. Now, if you have a safe in here, would you mind opening it, or should we drill?"

Marcuso opened his wall safe and sat and watched, read the search warrant and had an intense conversation with his legal department, as Finch and the two officers went through its contents and then started on the desk, pulling out each drawer so that nothing could be concealed in, behind or under it. Each book was removed from the bookcase and fanned, and each smiling Marcuso on a magazine cover was removed from the wall and disassembled. Every square inch of the office was searched for anything larger than an envelope.

"Where does that door lead?" Finch asked.

"It's a private bathroom," Marcuso answered.

Finch opened the door to a little room with the same wood paneling as the office but with plumbing. As he surveyed the space for any conceivable hiding place, one of the officers spoke over his shoulder. "You smell that?"

Finch sniffed the air and nodded. "Smells like a wet campfire in here," he said, as he noticed the metal wastebasket near the sink. It seemed out of place in the elegant little room. Its bottom was coated with a black, carbon substance that was still a little soft to the touch. Finch produced a plastic trash bag, put the wastebasket inside, sealed and labeled it. A tiny spider scurried into the folds of the plastic.

Finch said, "I think we're through."

Marcuso didn't show them out.

Finch handed the trash bag to one of the officers. "Take this on down and get it to the lab. I'm going to get Sirkel."

At Emory Sirkel's office, the fish face secretary seemed a little too happy to say, "He's not in."

"So," Finch said, "where is he?"

She pursed her big lips and shook her head. "Somewhere in the casino," she said. Then she saw the look on Finch's face, held up one finger, and picked up her phone for a quick conversation. "He's in the poker area," she said.

# Chapter Forty Seven

The dealer dealt the next hand. Phil was the big blind.

Mikey looked at his cards and bet $5,000. J. C. matched it. Veejay bet $10,000. Audra Sue folded. Phil threw in his cards like throwing stars.

"Can't do crap without cards," he said, "and enough chips to play."

"You can't seem to do crap with them," J. C. said.

"I got something for you," Phil said, holding up a freeway finger.

J. C. glanced at Audra Sue and shook his head. "I think someone skipped his anger management classes," he said.

"My daddy used to say asses should be seen—not heard," Audra Sue said.

"Sarcasm!" Phil said. "Yet another service she offers."

The play shifted to Mikey. His hand was covering his ear and his mouth was moving. Then, another one of those things happened that would not have occurred in Sioux Falls or even Des Moines, or, for that matter, probably anywhere else but Vegas. With all the other noise in the casino you might not have heard the dull thud from the parking lot, but Mikey let out a loud "FUCK!" and fell right out of his chair to writhe on the floor. He was ripping at his ear as he continued to roll and holler. Security launched themselves from all points in the casino as Berta Mae flung herself, quite a dangerous maneuver, onto the floor with Mikey. Some observers would later say that she was consoling him; others would say she was just trying to make him shut up. "Hush, Cheeso, hush! Cheeso! Cheeso!" Regardless, she half smothered him into relative quiet. Mikey finally dug what appeared to be a pink ball of wax from his ear and looked at it as if it were a poisonous snake that had just bitten him. He threw it toward the blackjack pit, the sound of plastic explosive, bursting gastank and shredding metal still ringing in his ear. A drop of blood ran down his left lobe.

Security walkie-talkies crackled and the full extent of the damage was soon being discussed all over the casino. The details would be on the evening news. With helicopter shots.

A big black SUV parked in "handicapped" had suddenly blown up, and the force of the explosion had lifted the white van parked by its side. The van arched upward and dropped squarely, but upside down, on a little four door sedan, covered with yellow magnetic ribbons and a "Just Married" sign. As tourist cameras rolled, a dark complexioned man with wires hanging off of him crawled out the back of the van and sprinted toward the Strip, but not before the owners of the sedan arrived, the elderly lady screaming "If you're so handicapped, how can you run so damn fast?," reigniting that ageless controversy at local domino games, while throwing, boomerang style, yellow magnetic ribbons at the fleeing man. One nearly took his ear off.

Spike and Oxxie were not smiling. Spike said, "I ain't going back near that damn dog."

Meanwhile, Mikey lay in a heap on the floor, and, although his apparent ear attack had corresponded to the car bombing, there was no reason at that point to make the connection.

"What in the hell happened?" J. C. asked Berta Mae. She was short of breath and growing even shorter on patience.

"Seizure," she said.

"Wow," J. C. said, "he's got some major health issues."

"Most men do," Berta Mae said. "Are you in good health?"

Mikey pulled himself together and climbed back onto his chair, working his jaw back and forth in an attempt to restore his hearing, and said, "Fuck. Now, where da fuck were we?" Mikey looked at his cards again, looked at J. C., and then said "Fold."

J. C. turned to Veejay. "It's a tell. If he falls on the floor again, that means he's got nothing." Then, J. C. said, "All in."

The bartender took that moment to deliver the drinks, and he bent over and whispered to Audra Sue as he put her Mimosa in front of her.

Before Veejay could bet, Audra Sue said, "New Delhi. Is that a monarchy?"

Veejay turned his head sharply. "No," he answered. "Parliamentary." He then looked at the dealer and said, "I fold." J. C.'s two Kings won but were sorely shortchanged.

Harrison Finch said, "You're under arrest . . ."

And Berta Mae's eyes got big, then she leaned over against a casino column for the inevitable weapons frisk. Mikey was reaching for his cell phone to call his lawyer. J. C. froze in place, while Audra Sue's face turned crimson. Spike dived under a slot machine. The dealer pulled a plastic baggy from his pants and dropped it under the table.

Emory Sirkel turned around to face Finch. He'd been standing by the table changing the channels on a hand-held T.V. "Are you talking to me?" he said.

"Mr. Sirkel, come with me and I'll read your Miranda rights on the way to the car," Finch said.

"You're arresting me?" Sirkel asked, and then that conversation and the two men faded into the commotion of the casino as the table tried to recover with deep breaths and a couple of nervous laughs.

The dealer turned to Mikey. "Your blind," he said.

Mikey nodded, "Fuckin' deaf, too," as he put $1000 on the table.

J. C. folded because Little Bobby told him to fold.

Veejay folded, on his own.

Audra Sue folded after glancing over toward the bartender who was holding a fist into the air. Phil looked that way and the fist turned into a friendly wave.

Phil bet $5000.

Mikey, sans Cholo, and, what he did not know, sans SUV, folded.

Phil turned over his two pocket Aces. "You know, these ought to be worth more than $1000," he said, "and they would be if something wasn't going on here! How did you all know I had these Aces?"

Little Bobby whispered into J. C.'s ear, "What's going down?"

"Fuckin' what?" Mikey said. "Whatja fuckin' sayin'?"

"I'm saying, Chee-Sooo," Phil said, "everybody here seems to know everyone else's hole cards, and that's no good for my game, and it's not going to be good for your health if I see how you're doing it."

"You fuck," Mikey said, getting up.

"Relax," J. C. said, raising a palm toward Mikey to keep him seated. "Let's just finish the game, guys."

"Da maggot call me Cheeso one more fuckin' time, he'll be fuckin' wid da fishes," Mikey said, pointing at Phil.

Phil lowered his sunglasses so he could glare at Mikey over the top of them. Mikey slowly sat down, but it was far from an act of surrender.

Oxxie said, "Uh oh. Dead man playing."

Spike said, "Maybe Mikey will hire us to blow the guy up."

"We the experts," Oxxie said.

Mikey posted the small blind, J. C. the big blind, and the game continued.

Veejay bet $5000. "The big dog's holding two Queens," Little Bobby transmitted to J. C.

Audra Sue glanced toward the bar and folded.

Phil went "all in," then got out of his seat to watch the action.

Mikey folded.

Little Bobby said, "The guy on the end has the big slick, Ace and King of Spades. I don't think this is your battle." J. C. agreed and folded.

The bartender walked up. "M'am," he said to Audra Sue, "can I get you something from the bar?"

Audra Sue hesitated, then said, "Why don't you make a suggestion?"

The bartender said, "Well, we have two of the best scotches made."

Veejay turned his eyes toward the bartender and managed a discreet nod, but not discreet enough for Phil.

"Okay!" Phil shouted, still standing, "Did everyone hear that? Did you see that? They're talking code over here. I got everything I own on the damn table and they're standing here talking about what I have!" He motioned for the table host. "Hey, moron. Did you hear that?"

The table host coughed and kept writing on a tally pad.

J. C. said, "I didn't hear anything." He turned to Mikey. "Did you hear anything?"

"Fuck no," Mikey said. Then, to Phil, "Why donja shut da fuck up?!"

Phil pulled his service revolver from his jacket and tossed his sunglasses aside.

"F.B.I.," Phil said, "you're all under arrest!"

"F.B.I.?" J. C. said.

"You fuck!" Mikey said.

Phil pointed the gun at Mikey who pulled his own gun, a little silver .22, and shot Phil. Everyone, including Little Bobby, gasped, as Phil grabbed his chest and they watched him slump onto his knees and down toward the table. Then another shot, much louder, sent the players scurrying for cover. Only Mikey stood there, staring at Berta Mae, as she stared at the .357 magnum she was holding, smoke wisping from the barrel. Oxxie unwrapped his arms from around her middle and stepped away quickly.

"Fuckin' whore," Mikey said, eyes wide on Berta Mae, as he touched the hole in his chest and then fell forward, scattering his chips, face first onto the table.

# Chapter Forty Eight

Berta Mae was led into a room with four metal walls. Still handicuffed, she was directed to sit at a small rectangular table in a chair with green, time-split cushions. A heavy steel door rolled open and Harrison Finch stepped inside the room, a hint of a smile on his face.

"The jailer said you need to see me," Finch said.

"I didn't kill Mikey," Berta Mae said.

"That's why you wanted to see me? To tell me you're innocent?" Finch said. "Do you know how much I hear that?"

"I'm serious, Detective Finch. I didn't kill him."

"Well, there are about thirty witnesses saying something different. They looked around when they heard the shot, saw you with the gun, and Mikey was cursing you for shooting him," Finch said.

"So they didn't actually see me shoot him!"

"That's for your lawyer to argue."

"I was thinking, what about the casino cameras? Don't they tape everything in those places?" Berta Mae said.

"I looked at the tapes."

"And what did you see? I know you didn't see me shoot Mikey!" Berta Mae said.

Harrison Finch took a deep breath and decided to answer. "There are three cameras. One is set for a broad view of the table and the other two can move around. One camera was on the first victim, Phillip Riley, and the other one was on Mikey, because of what was going on. The broad range camera isn't a close up shot, and everyone is crowded in, but it shows you there with the gun. Look, Berta Mae, I'm not sure why you wanted to see me. I can stand here and discuss our case with you all day, but I see no point in that. Tell me your story, or let's get you a lawyer in here and you can make a formal statement."

"You mean a confession?" Berta Mae asked.

"If you want to confess I'm sure that'll help you. If you want to confess to some of the other murders you're responsible for, maybe we can work up some sort of package deal," Finch explained.

"I don't want to *confess*!" Berta Mae said, rattling her handcuffs against the table. "I want to tell you what really happened!"

"Okay," Finch said, sitting across from Berta Mae at the table, "I'll give you about five minutes. You want a lawyer?"

"Nah. Lawyers suck. I've been married to three. It was the worst year of my life."

"Tell me what happened in the casino."

"Well, I'm standing there, watching the poker game, and this guy at the end of the table . . ."

"The one directly across from Mikey?"

"Yeah. This guy's getting madder and madder. Says he's being cheated. Says everyone knows his hole cards."

"Saying this to Mikey?" Finch asked.

"Not especially. Accusing everyone of talking in code and things like that. All of a sudden he jumps up and pulls out a gun, says 'I'm with the F.B.I. and you're all under arrest,' something like that. Mikey sees the gun, I don't know whether he heard the guy or not, because he was having trouble with one of his ears, and he shoots the guy."

"You saw that," Finch said.

"Yeah, then somebody—somebody really big—wraps his arms around me and I look down as this big gun goes off right in front of me like a cannon. I guess I grabbed it, like, involuntarily. I don't know why—maybe to keep it from turning toward me. And then there I stand, and Mikey's looking at me . . . like I just shot him. That was the last thought he ever had." Berta Mae buried her head in her hands and sobbed real tears.

"Because there you stood, holding the smoking gun," Finch said.

"I'd never shoot Mikey! Won't anyone believe that?" Berta Mae cried.

"Berta Mae," Finch said, "I think you've stretched that old rubber cord of belief pretty thin."

"You don't see anyone on the tape with his arms around me?"

"I told you, everybody's real close up, and there's a lot of confusion, people running and flailing this way and that when the first shot was fired. Even before that—when Riley showed his pistol. People even ducking behind other people. Probably some folks hoping their husband would take a bullet." Finch chuckled, but Berta Mae didn't seem to get the joke. "In all honesty, this whole thing's pretty strange: why you'd shoot Mikey at all, why you'd shoot him in front of all those people and knowing you were in a security area as tight as the White House, and I think I do recall from the tape a really big guy right up behind you at one point, but the angle's all wrong to corroborate your story. We're just going on what the eyewitnesses say. Nobody's said anything about this big guy you're talking about. Nobody says anybody else fired the gun. They said the gun was out in front of you when the shot went off. I don't know what else to believe."

"But they didn't actually see me shoot."

"They saw enough," Finch said.

Berta Mae let out an exasperated breath. "So," wiping her handcuffed wrists down her damp cheeks, "what are we looking at?"

"First degree murder," Finch said with a shrug. "Carries twenty to life. He had a gun, and he'd actually fired it, so you might be able to raise a self defense issue, or maybe defense of a third person, but the jury's going to hear about those husbands, Berta Mae."

Berta Mae got very quiet, sat very still, her eyes on her hands. "You said something about a 'package deal?'"

"I can't promise you anything. I'd have to get everything approved through the District Attorney."

Berta Mae nodded her understanding. "But what do you think?"

Finch leaned back in his chair and folded his arms. "Just tell me this, Berta Mae. You ready to come clean on those five husbands we talked about?"

"Including Alex Sharp?" Berta Mae said.

"Especially Alex Sharp," Finch said, "and you'd have to tell me how you got the information on the bungee cord."

"I can tell you that right now," Berta Mae said.

"I think I already know," Finch said.

"I was married to this guy . . ."

"Big Bobby Crest," Finch said.

"Who? Oh, yeah, I was married to him, too. No, I was married to this little round guy by the name of Emory Sirkel. He worked there at the casino and had a real bitch with Victor Marcuso. Thought he was smarter than Marcuso and kept looking for ways to prove it."

"Berta Mae," Finch said, "I think you may have just opened up some options."

# Chapter Forty Nine

"Jesus, Harry, you've been busy," Shauna Tell said, pouring him a paper cup of coffee from the break room pot.

Harrison Finch wrapped around a little linoleum topped table that someone had picked up at Goodwill. "We got Berta Mae Pole," he said, "killing Mikey right there in front of everybody."

"He needed killing," Shauna added. "Is that her defense?"

"Her defense is that someone else reached around her and pulled the trigger. It could be true."

"My god! I wouldn't believe that if I saw it in a movie," Shauna said.

"Frankly, that makes better sense than what happened, but, the way I look at it, let a jury decide. If they get her off the street they'll have done a good deed for everybody."

"None of your Diogenes bullshit on this one? Turn off the light, the party's over?"

"It bothers me, but, you know, I'm kind of sick and tired of American justice—let's have a little natural justice. She's an evil person."

"And evil has befallen her," Shauna said, sitting with her own cup, sipping it carefully, thoughtfully, but really just because it was hot.

"Something like that."

"How is our befallen F.B.I. agent?" Shauna asked.

"Better. That .22 slug hit a rib and ricocheted through both lungs. Missed his heart by an inch. He was breathing blood by the time they got him to the hospital, but he'll live. Old Herb Cox down at the Bureau said he'd shot the kid himself if he'd known he was in a casino."

"And Herb's a better shot than Mikey," Shauna said.

"The weird thing . . . ," Finch started.

"The weird thing? Like none of the rest of this is the least bit odd?"

"The weird thing is what the lab found," Finch said.

"Oh, yeah, I heard something about that."

"They take this muck out of the bottom of Marcuso's waste basket and it is a paper product, burned with some kind of igniter, like charcoal starter fluid. But it's burned up; they can't reconstruct it. So, Mingus, that strange little guy in the lab?"

"The one that has the hots for you?" Shauna asked.

"Damn it, Shauna. He notices all these little spiders on the can and even on the bag we delivered it in. He takes some samples. Mingus said it was some sort of wood spider that lives in damp places, and Marcuso's office didn't sound like a natural habitat. So, I tell him about Bobby Crest, and he goes over to Bobby Crest's house, must have freaked the poor kid out, gets permission to go up into the attic, and, sure enough, there's this same breed of spider."

"So, Marcuso's goin' down on a spider's D.N.A., is that what you're telling me? Is that beautiful, or what?"

"The spider makes the connection between the files and Marcuso's burned up waste can. Surely you can sell that to a jury!"

"What webs we weave. You know, I'd like to switch jobs for a while. You come down and do the selling—I'll do the collecting," Shauna said.

"There's not a jury this side of La-La Land that'd let Marcuso go on that evidence."

"Why are you worried about Marcuso if we got such a strong hook in Emory Sirkel?" Shauna asked. "Sirkel's going to roll on everyone. He's built to roll!"

"Yeah, well, we'll see. Apparently, there's some real bad blood between Sirkel and Marcuso. Both of them are pointing the finger at the other one. And now, Sirkel's hired the Dream Team and saying Berta Mae Pole is an opportunistic bitch."

"Which we already knew."

"Right, but she's our opportunistic bitch. We need her if we're going to jack a simple little obstruction of justice case up to a homicide."

"You know Marcuso and Sirkel will probably never spend a day in jail," Shauna said, her coffee was cooled off so she was probably sipping thoughtfully.

Finch unwound himself from the little table and stood up, crushing and tossing the paper cup in a nearby receptacle. "Yeah, but neither one will ever work in dis bidness again."

"And that's important to you?" Shauna asked.

"I look at it this way," Finch said. "If at sundown, the streets are cleaner, I've done my job."

"Jesus, Harry, you need a vacation!"

# Chapter Fifty

Spike and Oxxie drove hard toward a Caribbean island.

Oxxie read the brochure. "Listen to this," he said, "Middle America, between Nicaragua and Panama, bordering both the Caribbean Sea and the North Pacific Ocean."

"Kansas?" Spike guessed.

"Costa Rica," Oxxie said, "and they got forests down there so I won't look so conspicuous." Oxxie wore his Big Foot suit. Traveling incognito.

"Can we drive there?" Spike asked.

"Easier than Haiti," Oxxie said, "and their extradition laws are about the same."

"You're saying," Spike said, emphatically, "that I can go down to this Costa Rica place, go out on the beach in my red thong swim suit, and nobody can pick me up and bring me back to the States?"

"Nobody's going to pick you up in that red thong," Oxxie said.

"Well," Spike said, gesturing toward the space in front of his head like he was shooing no-see-ums, "that's a . . ."

"You're looking for a word, aren't you, Spike?"

"That's . . ."

"Don't Spike."

"That's nirvana, that's, uh, Shangri-La, that's . . ."

"I'm begging you, Spike."

"That's an idyllic, paradisiacal, place."

"Spike, you're hung like Einstein and smart as a horse," Oxxie said.

"What?" Spike said, touching his tongue to his upper lip.

"I saw that on that car up there," pointing, "hung like Einstein and smart as a horse. See? Maybe I should start collecting bumper stickers. Look at that one: my son's a trustee at the county jail. Must be a Democrat."

"That's not what that says, Oxxie."

Oxxie bumped the car onto a dirt road off the main two-lane. "Whoa," Spike said, "where in the hell are we going?"

"Shortcut."

"Shortcut? To Costa Rica?"

The road finally ended at a little circular patch of yucca and mesquite. Oxxie glanced over at Spike when they stopped, who was staring straight out of the windshield like he knew what was coming.

"Spike," Oxxie said, "I'm sorry to have to do this."

Oxxie reached down beside his seat and opened his door, and a slick black shape with shiny pearl teeth leapt over his legs and landed in the middle of the seat, between Oxxie and Spike. Panting.

Spike opened his mouth and screamed.

"Honeypie ran away from home," Oxxie said.

"So we're taking her back," Spike stopped screaming long enough to say. Honeypie twisted her head and bit his shoulder.

"No, Spike, we're taking her with us."

A low gutteral purr came from Honeypie, which changed to a growl when she looked at Spike.

"What about Scary Larry?" Spike asked.

"He's not good to her. Too much flossing."

"So he ran her off?" Spike asked.

"He doesn't know yet," Oxxie said.

"So now he'll chase us down and blow us up!" Spike said.

"For Honeypie, it's a chance we'll have to take."

Honeypie smiled, then took another swipe at Spike.

# Chapter Fifty One

"Goodbye, again," Audra Sue said.

The bartender pointed Audra Sue toward a table and poured two quick Mimosas to join her there. "A toast," he said, raising his glass, "to saving the whale."

Audra Sue clinked. "He's probably halfway back to India by now, with tales of outlaws and shootouts."

The bartender pulled a roll of green halfway out of his pants pocket. "I met him in the pool . . ."

"No, you didn't!"

"I met him in his *room* while they still had the casino doors locked taking glamour shots of Mikey. He said we probably saved him $40,000, so he gave it all to us," the bartender said.

"All of it?" Audra Sue asked. "He didn't get rich by giving his money away."

"I don't think he wanted anything to do with it. He said something about bad karma. 'The sum of a man's actions in his current existence will affect his future fate.' Besides, I told him I'd help him out as soon as the table's back up and running."

"You'll both come back as grasshoppers."

"Green grasshoppers."

"Hasn't that table caused enough trouble?" Audra Sue asked.

"Not yet."

"Well," Audra Sue said, reaching for her purse, "we doubled our money. We need to settle up."

"Consider us settled," the bartender said.

"What? Half of this $60,000 is yours," Audra Sue said.

"Yeah, and half of this money," the bartender patted his pocket, "is yours. I say we call it even. 60-40 because you were in the line of fire," the bartender said.

"Thanks," Audra Sue said, "I mean it."

"Are you going to L.A.?" the bartender asked.

"I think so," Audra Sue answered.

"We'll miss you. Of course, if you go, you won't be able to play that game tomorrow night."

Audra Sue had her purse and was rising. "What game?" she asked, sitting slowly.

"Oh, they've got a women's qualifier. Entry fee of $10,000. Winner gets a trip to the Bahamas to play in the big tournament next month, with a couple of million at stake."

"Are you suggesting what I think you're suggesting?" Audra Sue asked.

"What am I suggesting—I mean what are you thinking I'm suggesting? I mean, what do you think I'm . . ."

"Shut up. That we might be able to take advantage of our favorite table?" Audra Sue asked.

"Cheat?!" the bartender said, in falsetto. "I just thought you might want to play, sounds like a great opportunity, and if you look over here occasionally, and I wave, or I bring you a Mimosa or two, so what? It's a free world."

Audra Sue clasped her purse tightly in both hands, a squinched-up smile on her face like someone was about to hit her. "I dunno," she said, hoping if she fell, there'd be a net. There always seemed to be a net.

# Chapter Fifty Two

J. C. sprawled on the couch. Little Bobby paced, eyes shut.

"God!" Little Bobby said. "That lab guy really freaked me out. If they want spiders I can give them spiders. I think I slept in a damn nest of them last night. Slept? Did I say 'slept?' I didn't sleep a wink. All night long I kept thinking, 'someone's going to come through that door and haul me off to the desert.' Then that guy gets murdered right there at the table . . ."

"Bobby Bobby Bobby. It's over. We're out of there in one piece. No harm done," J. C. said.

"No harm done?! One guy's in the morgue and another one's in I.C.U.! We didn't win any money and the police are coming in and out of my house arresting my spiders!"

J. C. laughed out loud. "Don't you have any regular medication you take?"

"Get out of my house!" Little Bobby stopped pacing and pointed a long arm toward the door. "Just get out right now!"

"Just let me say this," J. C. said, holding up his index finger, still comfortable on the couch, "I agree with you, the table's too hot. We can't play on it again."

"My god," pacing again. "What a concession! Will you also agree the world is round?"

"What we can do, though, is find out if there are tables at other casinos."

"*You* can, J. C. I don't want anything else to do with this," waving his arms.

"Well, you're hysterical right now, and I think it'd be a good idea if you'd calm down and think about . . ."

"J. C.! I'm not thinking about anything!"

"Okay," J. C. said, "What about this . . ."

"NOOOO!" Little Bobby turned and ran down the hall. A door slammed.

J. C. got off the couch and headed toward the bathroom door, stopping briefly to pull a beer out of the refrigerator. He knocked on the bathroom door. "Bob-by? I haven't talked to someone through a bathroom door since I asked my girlfriend if the baby was mine. I have something to tell you, Bobby."

A muffled, "What?"

"While you were spending the night at the casino I had a chance to read your prospectus. The one you had to redo after Marcuso tossed out your only copy."

Silence. Then a throaty, "Uh huh."

"I like it."

Several minutes could have passed. The door creaked open, wide enough for Bobby's half-shut eye. "You liked it?"

J. C. turned and walked away as he said, "Greensox. I like it. Vegas needs a major league team."

Little Bobby followed him, gobbling down every word in J. C.'s wake.

"The problem," J. C. said, opening the refrigerator and handing Little Bobby a beer, "is getting it in the hands of someone who can make it happen. I know this guy, big sports fanatic, got more money than God, I'd like to pitch the deal to him and see what he says."

"Okay."

"What I'm thinking, let's run over to the Schaherazod, check out their tables. Now, hold it! Don't freak out on me! We check out their tables; see if we can get a picture on the T.V., and, if we do, we take the prospectus up state. Make a two for one deal. If the guy'll ramrod the team, we'll give him the scoop on the table. Just a little added incentive to get him interested. Make sense?"

Little Bobby shook his head. "I guess it's worth a try."

# Chapter Fifty Three

*On Eyewitness Now, Tonight, Emory Sirkel, former Chief of Operations of the Four Winds Hotel and Casino entered a plea of guilty today to intentional manslaughter and was sentenced to ten years in prison. The plea ended an extensive investigation by law enforcement officials . . .*

"Into the tragic death of Alex Sharp—whose rubber broke," the bartender finished the newscast and switched off the local news.

"Little bit of excitement around here."

"Oh, yeah. Scary. You need another one?" He picked a stemmed glass from the rack and poured another glass of merlot. "Yeah, our C.E.O. got booted, too. Emory Sirkel spun on everyone like a top."

"Sounds like Sirkel took a pretty stiff sentence. He must have thought a jury would hammer him."

"In my opinion, he was the bad guy. He actually helped to set up some poor snook to go off the bungee jump so his wife, Sirkel's ex-wife, could sue the casino. That's pretty damn cold. All Marcuso did was destroy the evidence."

"Not smart. If you get caught."

"What Marcuso didn't know was that The Sirkel had handed him a bunch of schematics on crooked poker tables at other casinos—that's what Sirkel told the Gaming Commission. But Marcuso burned the whole file. Probably didn't even look at the schematics. So the gaming commish drilled him a new one. Said he should have reported the tables. They revoked his gaming license for that *and* his criminal conviction and this place was run by a committee out of Carson City for three weeks. All because of some spider's D.N.A."

"A spider? I'm not sure I even want to know what that means. Whatever happened to that lady with the big boobs?"

"You just described a third of Vegas, dude, but, if you mean Berta Mae Pole, she's doing hard time. She went before the court on an open plea and boo-hooed real tears and sighed those big mountains up and down, to and fro, until she got a wide-eyed and probably very lonely judge to take mercy on her and give her twenty years. That means she'll be eligible for parole in seven. Now, the legislature's debating whether to limit how many times a person can get married.

The A.C.L.U. will have a heyday with that one, but I tend to agree. After twenty trips to the alter, you ought to quit. Or just live in sin."

"How did the D.A. feel about Berta Mae getting off so easy?"

"The one who was really pissed was the detective on the case, Harrison Finch. He went over to her lawyer's office, Fitzlow Everhard, and raised all kinds of hell. They had to carry ol' Fitzlow off to the hospital."

"My god! Finch beat him up?"

"No, Fitzlow got a nosebleed when Finch mentioned that Berta Mae was once married to her sentencing judge and that the Bar Association might be interested in knowing that."

"Is that true?"

"I don't know."

"Fitzlow—the one who wears a cape?"

"Yeah. I do know Berta Mae was married to Big Bobby Crest. Did you know Big Bobby?" the bartender asked.

"Played poker with him."

"And you probably lost. His son's still in town. Saying he can get us a baseball expansion team," the bartender said. "Hooked up with some guys upstate but it sounds like a pipedream."

"Sounds just like Big Bobby."

"Chip off the ol' block. Some ad man from New York was involved with all that, but he caught a little hitch here recently when he and a dude they call Cholo got busted over at the Schaherazod for cheating. He and Bobby cut ties. With all the easy money to be made out here in Vegas, who needs to cheat?" the bartender asked. "Anyway, the ad man headed back east, he and that Cholo guy. Maybe they'll find the Atlantic City casinos more 'receptive.'"

"Weren't they involved in that shooting? The gangster and that F.B.I. guy?"

"Indirectly. The ad man was playing right next to Mikey Mozzarelli when he died. The last time anyone saw Phil Riley, that F.B.I. guy? He was getting thrown off an Indian casino."

"Told to leave?"

"No. Tossed. Like a trash bag. Into the Red River. Hey," the bartender said, "wait a minute." The bartender turned up the sound on the T.V.

*In other news, amateur poker player Audra Sue Dunn of Marcusville, Oklahoma beat out a final table of some of the best women poker players in the world today on Paradise Island in the Bahamas, taking home a final pot of over two million dollars. When asked how she felt about her amazing, come from behind victory, she said, "I won't stop until I wear the national bracelet!"*

The bartender whistled. "Maybe she didn't need any help."

*Finally, this report just in from the Caribbean island of Aruba. Today was the second day of multiple sightings of what islanders are calling Mucho Basa, a huge, hairy creature romping among the coconut palms of their tropical paradise closely followed by several island dogs. . . .*

The bartender turned off the set. "You want another one? You know, as long as you're sticking quarters into that video poker game, the drinks are on the house, my man. Maybe you'd try one of my famous boat drinks from my new blender?"

"A lot of sugar in those?"

"Probably."

"Bad for the ga'damn teeth," Scary Larry said.

One last postscript.

Some months later, a baby boy was born in a prison infirmary. A nurse, who was simply never informed of how the child's father had died, referred to him as a "bouncing baby boy." The Rag later picked that up as a headline. His Christian name was Alex, but, to Berta Mae, he'd always be nicknamed Cheeso.

He had enough money in the trust fund created for him by the Four Winds to become an arrogant, lazy, but well-groomed adult, or a politician. Instead, he became the best shortstop who ever played for the Las Vegas Greensox.

BVG